Do you ever
som

In Her Shoes

Modern-day Cinderellas get their grooms!

Now you can with Harlequin Romance®'s
miniseries brimming full of contemporary,
feel-good stories, as modern-day Cinderellas
swap glass slippers for stylish stilettos!

So follow each footstep through makeover to
marriage, rags to riches, as these women fulfill
their hopes and dreams....

Step into Geena's shoes in

The Rancher's Housekeeper

by

Rebecca Winters

July 2012

Dear Reader,

Have you ever been accused of something you didn't do?

Every so often the media tells us about people who have spent time in prison for a crime they didn't commit. The possibility of that happening is a terrifying thought. No one can know their anguish before they're freed, or their joy when the mistake is caught and the injustice rectified.

I explored this idea in my latest novel, *The Rancher's Housekeeper*. Walk in Geena's shoes. You'll feel chills and then thrills when she meets the owner of the Floral Valley Ranch.

Enjoy!

Rebecca Winters

REBECCA WINTERS

The Rancher's Housekeeper

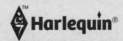

TORONTO NEW YORK LONDON
AMSTERDAM PARIS SYDNEY HAMBURG
STOCKHOLM ATHENS TOKYO MILAN MADRID
PRAGUE WARSAW BUDAPEST AUCKLAND

Recycling programs
for this product may
not exist in your area.

ISBN-13: 978-0-373-17817-9

THE RANCHER'S HOUSEKEEPER

First North American Publication 2012

Copyright © 2012 by Rebecca Winters

Rebecca Winters, whose family of four children has now swelled to include five beautiful grandchildren, lives in Salt Lake City, Utah, in the land of the Rocky Mountains. With canyons and high alpine meadows full of wildflowers, she never runs out of places to explore. They, plus her favourite vacation spots in Europe, often end up as backgrounds for her romance novels, because writing is her passion, along with her family and church.

Rebecca loves to hear from readers. If you wish to email her, please visit her website, www.cleanromances.com.

Books by Rebecca Winters

ACCIDENTALLY PREGNANT!
THE NANNY AND THE CEO
HER DESERT PRINCE
HER ITALIAN SOLDIER
A BRIDE FOR THE ISLAND PRINCE

Other titles by this author available in ebook format.

CHAPTER ONE

Colt Brannigan kissed his mother on the cheek. "I'll see you tonight." He turned to her caregiver. "I'm working with the nursing service in Sundance. They'll be sending someone out in the next few days to start helping you with Mom's care."

"I'll be fine. Hank's been able to give me some free time."

"That's good. See you tonight, Ina."

Colt's sixty-year-old mother didn't know anyone. She'd been diagnosed with Alzheimer's before his father's death sixteen months ago. It had grown much worse over the past year. She needed round-the-clock care.

"Hey, Colt?"

At the sound of his brother Hank's voice, Colt shut the bedroom door and strode down the hallway of the ranch house's main floor toward him.

"What's up?"

"Phone call for you from Warden James's office."

Warden James? "Must be a wrong number," he said, knowing full well it wasn't. He walked past his brother and headed for the back door, not needing another delay when he should be in the upper pasture.

Hank followed him at a slower pace due to his walking cast. "You *did* advertise for a housekeeper in the *Black Hills Sentinel*. They want to know if you've already filled the position."

Colt realized he should have indicated in the ad that they were looking for a female housekeeper. His mother would insist on it *if* she could express herself, but that time would never come again. "Tell them it's too late."

"But—"

"No buts!" He cut his brother off with a grimace. Before their father had passed away from blood clots in the lungs, he'd obliged the warden by granting him a favor, one he'd lived to regret.

The freed inmate had been taken on as a ranch hand on a provisional basis. He'd stayed only long enough for a few meals and a paycheck before he took off with the blanket from his bunk and some of the other hands' cash. To add injury to insult, he'd stolen one of the ranch's quarter horses.

Colt had tracked him down and recovered the stolen property. The ex-felon was once again behind bars. Unfortunately the percentage of freed inmates who ended up back in prison was high. Now that Colt ran the Floral Valley Ranch, he'd be damned if he would make the mistake his father had and invest any more time or money on an ex-con.

"I'll be checking fences all day. Won't be home until late. Call if there's an emergency." He jumped off the back porch and headed for the barn. After swinging into the saddle, he galloped away on Digger.

It took the right kind of female to run a household like theirs and manage the domestic help. In fact it took a *saint*, but those were in short supply since their previous housekeeper, Mary White Bird, had died. Colt realized their family could never replace her. The full-blooded Lakota had been their mother's right hand and an institution on the ranch.

He'd advertised in various newspapers throughout Wyoming and South Dakota, but so far none of the applicants had the qualifications he was looking for. Forget a released felon. Colt was getting desperate, but not *that* desperate.

Floral Valley Ranch 4 miles.

Geena Williams rode past the small highway sign and had to turn around. Eight miles back an old rancher at the Cattlemen's Stock and Feed Store in Sundance, Wyoming, had told her she might miss the turnoff if she weren't looking for it. He'd been right. From here on out it would be dirt road.

She stopped long enough to catch her breath and take a drink from her water bottle. During the day the temperature had been sixty-nine degrees, with some wind in the afternoon, typical for early June in northeastern Wyoming. But now it had dropped into the fifties and would go lower. Her second-hand parka provided little insulation.

Though the weather had cooperated, it was sheer will and adrenaline that had gotten her this far. Now desperation would have to get her the rest of the way. Her legs would probably turn to rubber before she reached her destination, but Geena couldn't quit now. She needed to make it to the ranch before it was too dark to see.

A half hour later she caught sight of a cluster of outbuildings, including the ranch house, but it was ten to ten and she didn't dare approach anyone this late.

She pedaled her road bike over to a stand of pines and propped it against one of the trunks.

Her backpack contained everything in the world she owned. No. That wasn't exactly true. There were some other items precious to her, but she had no idea where they were. Not yet anyway.

She undid the straps to eat some snacks. They tasted good. After she'd pulled out her space blanket, she more or less collapsed from exhaustion onto a soft nest of needles beneath the boughs of the biggest tree.

Using her pack for a pillow, she curled on her right side and covered up, still in shock that tonight the only roof she had over her head was a canopy of stars. She picked out the Big Dipper. Venus was the bright star to the west.

Heaven.

"Come on, Titus. Time to go home."

Colt shut the barn door. The border collie raced ahead of him with more energy than he knew what to do with. Titus led a dog's perfect life. He was loved. He ran and worked all day, ate the food he wanted and had no worries. That's why he went to sleep deliriously happy and woke up happy.

As for Colt, he wouldn't describe himself happy in the delirious sense. He'd been in that state only one time. Falling in love at twenty-one had been easy when you'd been on the steer-wrestling circuit, winning prize money and dazzling your girl.

It was the happily-ever-after part he didn't have time to work on before she wanted out because a married man had ranching duties and she wasn't having fun anymore. Their eleven-month marriage had to have been some kind of record for the shortest one in Crook County, Wyoming.

At thirty-four years of age now, he recognized his mistake. They'd been too young and immature. It simply didn't work. Since then he'd dated women from time to time, but unless he met one who enriched the busy life he already led, he didn't see himself in a rush to get married again.

Suddenly the dog switched directions away from the ranch house, barking his head off. He hadn't gone far when he made that low growling sound that let Colt know they had an intruder on the property. Whether animal or human he couldn't tell yet.

As he hurried to catch up, he heard a woman's voice say, "Easy, boy," trying her best to soothe the black-and-white beast who'd hunted her down. He weighed only forty-five pounds, but in the dark his terrifying growl had clearly made her nervous.

Closer now, Colt could see why. The female on her feet beneath their granddaddy's ponderosa was wrapped in a space blanket that covered her head. She probably couldn't see anything. Enveloped like that, she presented a tall silhouette to Titus who couldn't quite make her out. Any mystery caused the dog to bark with much more excitement.

Against the trunk Colt glimpsed a brand-new road bike. Next to her feet he saw a backpack. "Quiet, Titus," he commanded the dog, who made a keening sound for having to obey and walked over to Colt.

If she was a nature lover, she was going about it the wrong way. "Are you all right, ma'am?"

"Y-yes," she stammered. "Thank you for calling him off. He startled me." She had an appealing voice. The fact that she didn't sound hysterical came as another surprise.

"What in the devil do you think you're doing sleeping out here in the dark?" The women of his acquaintance wouldn't have dreamed of doing anything so foolhardy. "Any animal could bother you, especially a mountain lion on the prowl."

She pulled the edges of the blanket tighter. The motion revealed her face. "I got here too late to disturb anyone, so I thought I'd rest under the tree."

"You came to this ranch specifically?"

"Yes, but I realize I'm trespassing. I'm sorry."

Her apology sounded genuine and she spoke in a cultured voice. What in blazes? He was taken aback by the whole situation. After a glimpse into hauntingly lovely eyes that gave him no answers, he took in a quick breath before picking up her backpack. It was unexpectedly light and had seen better days.

"For whatever reason you've come, I can't allow you to stay out here. Leave the bike and follow me. It'll be safe where it is."

"I don't want to intrude."

She'd already done a good job of it and had gotten his attention in a big way, but that was beside the point. "Nevertheless, you'll have to come with me. Let's go."

The three of them made an odd trio as they entered the back door of the house. He showed her through the mudroom, past the bathroom to the kitchen. Titus headed for his bowls of food and water. After that he would go to his bed in the den. Colt's father had been gone a long time, but Colt had a hunch the loyal dog was still waiting for his return. Maybe Titus wasn't that happy after all.

Colt put the woman's backpack by one of the kitchen chairs. Out of the corner of his eye he watched her remove the space blanket. She *was* tall, probably five foot nine. He'd thought it might be the blanket above her head that had added the inches. After folding it, she laid it on the oblong wood table, then took off her insubstantial parka. He imagined she was in her mid-twenties.

Except for white sneakers, everything she wore, from her jeans to her long-sleeved navy crew neck, looked well-worn and hung off her. The clothes must have originally been bought for a larger woman. Her brunette hair had been pulled back with an elastic in an uninspiring ponytail. No makeup, no jewelry.

He thought he might have seen her before and tried to imagine her features and figure with a little more flesh on her. Had she been ill? In profile or frontal view, her mouth looked too drawn, the hollows in her cheeks too pronounced, but the fact still remained he felt an unwanted attraction.

Two physical characteristics about her were remarkable. Great bone structure and eyes of inky blue. They looked disturbingly sad as they peered at him through lashes as dark as her brows and hair. Why sad, he couldn't begin to imagine.

If she'd been running away from a traumatic situation, she bore no bruises or wounds he could see. She stood there proud and unafraid, reminding him of an unfinished painting that needed more work before she came to full life. That in itself added an intriguing element.

"You're welcome to use the bathroom we just passed."

"Thank you. I'll do that. Please excuse me."

After she disappeared, he walked over to the counter, bemused by her femininity. She'd been endowed with more of it than most women.

Hank had made a fresh pot of coffee and had probably gone to their mother's bedroom to sit with her for a while. As Colt reached for a couple of mugs from the shelf, his intruder returned. He told her to sit down. "I can offer coffee. Would you like some, or does tea sound better?"

"Coffee, please."

Colt poured two cups. "Sugar? Cream?" he called over his shoulder.

"Please don't go to any trouble. Black is fine."

He doctored both and brought them to the table where she'd sat down at the end. "I laced yours anyway. You look like you could use a pick-me-up."

"You're right. Thank you, Mr...."

"Colt Brannigan." He drank some of his coffee.

She cradled the cup. With her eyes closed, she took several sips, almost as if she were making a memory. This puzzled him. He stood looking down at her until she'd finished it. In his opinion she needed a good square meal three times a day for the foreseeable future.

"How about telling me who you are."

Her eyelids fluttered open, still heavy from fatigue. "Geena Williams." This time he thought he remembered that name from somewhere, too. Eventually it would come to him.

"Well, Geena—perhaps if I made you a ham sandwich, more information might be forthcoming about where you've come from and why you showed up on our property."

"Please forgive me. I'm still trying to wake up." He'd never heard anyone sound more apologetic. She got to her feet. "I was just freed from the women's prison in Pierre, South Dakota, today and came all the way to your ranch. I'd hoped to interview for the live-in housekeeper position for a temporary period of time, but it took longer for me to get here than I'd supposed."

With those words, Colt felt as if he'd just been kicked in the gut by a wild mustang. In an instant everything about her made sense, starting with the call from the prison warden this morning. He must have believed she was trustworthy, yet the new bike propped beneath the tree didn't match her used clothing. Had she stolen it?

She's an ex-felon. With the realization came an inexplicable sense of disappointment.

"Is the position still open?" The hope in that question, as if his answer meant life and death to her, almost got to him.

He had to harden himself against it. "I'm afraid not."

All people had baggage, but anyone who spent time in prison carried a different kind. Colt was looking for a housekeeper who was like Mary White Bird. A wise woman who'd raised a family of her own, a woman who'd helped his mom run the affairs of the ranch house since he was a boy without being obtrusive. She'd had an instinct for handling the staff and guests, not to mention the hothead personalities within the immediate and extended Brannigan clan.

As for Geena Williams, she was too young. She'd done time. He had no idea what crime she'd committed, but he knew she could use counseling to rejoin the world outside prison walls. Who knew the battles going on inside her? Hiring her was out of the question.

Her eyes glazed, yet not one tear spilled from those dark lashes. "You've been very kind to me, but I realize I've made a big mistake in coming here without arranging for an appointment first."

He frowned. "As it happens, Warden James called here this morning hoping to make one for you. I asked my brother to tell him it had already been filled. It appears the two of you had a miscommunication. For your sake, I'm sorry the warden didn't say anything to you."

A look of confusion marred her features. "Warden James is a woman, but I didn't know she'd called you. After I was taken to her office yesterday morning, she informed me I'd be freed this morning. I guess she was trying to help me find work so I would have some place to stay.

"As soon as I could go to the prisoners' lounge last evening, I scanned the classified section of the *Rapid City Journal* looking for work and saw your ad. I noticed it had been listed a while ago and feared it might have already been filled, but I decided to take a chance anyway and came straight here."

Colt was astounded by everything she'd told him. His brother had said the warden had seen the ad in the *Black Hills Sentinel*. Even if this woman were telling the truth, it didn't matter. There was no job on the ranch available to her or any other inmate, but he was consumed by curiosity. Shifting his weight he asked, "Don't you have a spouse or a boyfriend who could help you?"

"I've never been married. One fellow I was dating before my imprisonment never came near or tried to reach me."

Colt surmised their relationship couldn't have been that solid in the first place. "You don't have relatives who could help you?"

A shadow darkened her features. "None."

None?

He raked his hair in bewilderment, unable to imagine it before he realized she could be lying about it. Maybe she was ashamed to go home. Colt hadn't been in her shoes, so it wasn't fair to judge.

"How did you know where to come?" The ad indicated only that the ranch was near Sundance, Wyoming. Twelve miles, in fact. He'd only listed a box number.

"I realize I was supposed to respond with an email, but I didn't have access to a computer. By the time the bus dropped me off this afternoon in Sundance where I'd decided to start looking for work, I figured that if someone knew where you lived, I'd just come straight here.

"So after I bought my bike at the shop, I rode over to the Cattlemen's Stock and Feed Store. Everyone working there said they knew Colt Brannigan, the head of the Floral Valley Ranch. The owner sang your praises for taking over after your father died and making it even more successful. Then this older rancher who was just leaving was kind enough to tell me where to find the turnoff for your ranch."

Colt was dumbfounded by her explanation and her resourcefulness, especially the fact that she'd bought a bike. He could always call there to verify she'd actually made the purchase. "You rode all the way here on the highway at night?"

"Yes, but it wasn't dark then. I need transportation to get around. Since I don't have a driver's license yet, I can't buy a junker car."

"Isn't a new bike expensive?"

"Yes, but the bike at the shop in Sundance was on sale for $530.00. They threw in the used helmet for ten dollars. I would have bought all new clothes, but after that I only had $160 left of the money I withdrew from my prison savings account. I spent some of it on food, the space blanket and my shoes."

He blinked. "You earned the money in prison, I presume."

"Yes. They pay twenty-five cents an hour. That resulted in forty dollars a month for the thirteen months I was incarcerated."

Thirteen months in hell. What crime had she committed?

Colt ran his thumb along his lower lip. "So you came out of there with $520.00?"

"Seven hundred actually. I worked some extra shifts and they also give you fifty dollars when you leave."

He would never again begrudge his taxpayer dollars going to an ex-felon who'd paid her debt to society and had been freed from prison. "So how much money do you have on you now to live on?"

"Ninety-two dollars. That's why I need a job so desperately. I'm a good cook. In prison I did every job from helping in the kitchen and cleaning to laundry and warehouse work, to hospital and dispensary duty and prison-ground cleanup. I'm a hard worker, Mr. Brannigan. If you called the prison, they'd tell you I put in forty-plus hours every week with no infractions. Do you know of anyone in this area who might be looking for help?"

Anyone?

She was looking at someone who needed a housekeeper and an additional caregiver for his mother as soon as yesterday!

He rubbed the back of his neck, pondering his shock that he would even consider the possibility of her working for him when he knew next to nothing about her except the worst. Though she was definitely a survivor, the culprit tugging at him was the vulnerability in those intense dark blue eyes.

Before he could formulate his thoughts, let alone give any kind of answer, Titus came flying through the kitchen to greet Hank, who'd just walked in the back door with Mandy. Their presence surprised Colt because he'd thought Hank was with their mother.

Colt had been so deep in conversation, he hadn't heard Mandy's car. Since Hank had broken his leg, she'd been the one chauffeuring him around.

She smiled. "Hey, Colt—"

"Hey yourself, Mandy." She was a cute smart blonde from Sundance who'd known Hank since high school, but as usual he had eyes for someone else. This time they'd ignited with interest after swerving to the very female stranger standing in the kitchen.

Taking the initiative, Colt said, "Geena Williams? This is my brother Hank and his friend Mandy Clark."

Everyone said hello and shook hands. Hank could see the backpack and space blanket. He was dying to ask questions, but Colt wasn't ready to answer them and said nothing to satisfy his brother's burning curiosity.

"We'll be in the family room," Hank eventually muttered before they disappeared with Titus at their heels.

Geena reached for her parka and put it on. "I know I'm intruding. If you wouldn't mind me sleeping in the back of one of those trucks parked outside, I'll be gone first thing in the morning."

Colt had already come to one decision. Ignoring her comment he said, "You've had a long day. Take the coat off, Geena. I'm going to fix you a sandwich and some soup before you go to bed in the guest room. Tomorrow will take care of itself."

He'd heard that saying all his life and wasn't exactly sure what it meant. However, he didn't want to do any more thinking tonight. What he ought to do was drive her into town and fix her up at a hotel, but he was bushed. At least that was the excuse he was telling himself for keeping her here. She could sleep in Mary's former quarters down the other hallway.

Geena had done a lot of dreaming in prison. It had been the only way to escape the bars confining her. But not even her imagination could have conjured the living reality of Colt Brannigan.

She didn't know such a man existed outside her fantasies. By the way the men at the Cattlemen's Store had described him, she'd thought he must have been older to be a legend already. But Geena estimated he was in his mid-thirties. There was no sign or mention of a wife.

When she'd first seen him beneath the kitchen light, the intelligence in those hazel eyes examining her came close to taking the last breath out of her. She stared back in disbelief at the ruggedly gorgeous male who was without question in total charge of his world. Tall, dark and handsome was a cliché women had used for years, but in her mind *he* could have been the one who'd inspired the words.

Yet, putting all of those qualities and attributes aside, it was his kindness to her that made him unique and set him above other men. Instead of throwing her off his property, he'd brought her inside and fed her, given her a beautiful room and bed to sleep in, even after she'd told him she'd just gotten out of prison.

In a daze over everything that had happened, Geena emerged from the bathroom wearing a clean bathrobe she'd found hanging on the back of the door. Smelling sweet and squeaky clean, she turned out the lights and padded over to the queen-sized bed. She'd taken a bath *and* a shower, luxuriating in the products he'd provided for her to use.

All day and evening she'd been doing things unassociated with prison for the first time in over a year. The taste of freedom was indescribable. No more feeling of doom. No more fear that every second of your life from now on would be lived in constant purgatory. No more prison smells, no more sounds during the night of other prisoners being sick, coughing, sobbing, raging or fighting with other inmates through the walls.

No more claustrophobic gray cell, no more clank of prison bars or guards telling you when, where and how you would live, how you would talk and answer. No more living in a enclave with women who wanted nothing to do with each other, who lived to be on the outside with a man again. If any of them could see Mr. Brannigan...

While she sat on the side of the bed to finish drying her hair with a fluffy yellow towel, she looked out the tall picture window. It took up close to a whole wall of the spacious bedroom with its cross-beamed ceiling. She'd purposely left the curtains open so she could see the full moon casting its light across the foot of the hand-carved wood bed.

The room was filled with Sioux artifacts; rugs of the Lakota tribe covered the hardwood floor. On one wall hung a Sioux tapestry in predominantly red colors. Over the bed was an authentic beaded Sioux tobacco bag.

After her host had accompanied her to the room and left, she'd walked over to study the dozen framed photographs placed on the dresser. They featured a short Lakota woman. In some she was alone, in others she stood surrounded by her native family, all of whom were in ceremonial dress. Whoever she was she held a place of great honor in this wonderful ranch house. Though modernized in parts, it had to have been built at least a hundred and fifty years ago.

When her hair was dry enough, Geena formed it into a braid that fell over one shoulder. Her last act was to set the clock-radio alarm for four in the morning. Then she was finally able to lie down on two comfy pillows and relax.

Mr. Brannigan had gone out of his way to feed her and make her comfortable for the night. Geena couldn't help but think of the man who'd been rescued by the Good Samaritan. His gratitude couldn't have been any greater than hers for Mr. Brannigan's goodness. As soon as she could, she would repay him.

For now her first priority was to get some sleep before she slipped out of the house at first light and pedaled back to Sundance. She'd wanted the housekeeper job here, but since that wasn't possible, she'd take any job that would give her a roof over her head. If nothing turned up in Sundance, she'd double back to Spearfish, South Dakota, and look there.

One way or the other she had to stay close to Rapid City, the place where she needed to begin the search for Janice Rigby, the woman who'd once lived with Geena's brother before disappearing. Before he'd died, he'd told Geena that Janice was expecting. If she'd had the baby, it might be Geena's only living relative. She ached for

the family she'd lost. To have a little nephew or niece…
Time was of the essence for Geena to find out.

Geena could probably get her old job back in Rapid
City with FossilMania, but she didn't dare. For the pres-
ent she needed to remain invisible to the people who'd
known her before she'd been arrested. One of them
might see her and alert Janice she was out of prison.
For some strange reason, Janice had never liked Geena.
She didn't want to frighten the other woman off before
Geena could catch up to her.

But she'd worry about all that tomorrow. For what
was left of the rest of the night she'd dream about Colt
Brannigan.

CHAPTER TWO

COLT entered the den and patted Titus's head. "I'm going to keep you company for a while." After closing the door, he moved over to the desk and sat down at the computer. Too wired to sleep right now, he typed the name *Gina Williams* in the search engine. She'd been in prison. There might be something about her from some old newspaper and magazine articles.

Nothing came up but a lot of other females whose profiles were online. He tried a different spelling. More of the same. On a whim he searched for a list of different spellings. Up came Jean, Geenah, Jeenah, Jina, Jeana, Geana, Ginah, Giena, Jiena, Gienah, Geena.

He tried each one. After putting in the last name on the list, he was ready to call it quits for the night when twenty entries popped up. All of them recounted the brutal slaying of Rupert Brown, an eighty-one-year-old widower of Rapid City, South Dakota. The collector of priceless Old West and Indian artifacts had been attacked and slain by *Geena* Williams, twenty-six, the tenant living in the basement apartment of his house.

Colt shot out of the chair, feeling as if he'd been the one stabbed. Geena had committed murder? *That* murder?

He rocked back on his cowboy boots, unable to believe it. While his mind and body were reeling, he grabbed the back of the chair until he could get a grip on his emotions, but adrenaline kept him on his feet.

He remembered hearing about the sensational murder on the evening news. The killer had been a beautiful young single woman. That's why she'd looked familiar to him.

Incredulous, he sank back down in the chair, damned if he read the rest, damned if he didn't. Compelled to finish, he read the entire article. Robbery had been the motive. It had happened soon after Colt's father had died and their family had been in deep mourning, but the story had been all over the media, so he had heard about it at the time.

He groaned loudly enough that Titus moved over and sat by him. Again Colt felt as though he'd been the one repeatedly bludgeoned with the Marshalltown trowel she'd plunged into the old man's chest numerous times.

Colt knew every human had a dark side, but to imagine that the woman sleeping in Mary's room had killed an old man in cold blood seemed beyond the realm of possibility to him.

There was a picture of her after she'd been taken into custody. She'd been fifteen to twenty pounds heavier then with hair to her shoulders. According to one of the reports, she'd been given sixty years. That was as good as a lifetime sentence.

But she'd served only thirteen months of it.... How could she be out on parole this fast? Had there been a mistrial? Some snag that had freed her because the evidence wasn't strong enough to hold her?

There had to be a flaw in Colt that had misread the

purity in her eyes. Geena had seemed like a shiny dime gleaming pure silver he'd picked up from the ground. But when he turned it over, he discovered rust had eaten the silver away.

Her situation reminded him of the freed prisoner his father had hired. His dad had felt sorry for the younger man. *Everyone makes mistakes, Colt. This man deserves a second chance.*

But the second chance had turned into an opportunity for the ex-felon to take advantage and rob his father.

Colt's instincts had been right not to hire this woman, but he wanted an explanation for Geena's release and he wanted it now!

Grabbing his phone, he called South Dakota information for the women's prison in Pierre. In a minute he was put through to the prison's voice mail. There was a menu. He pressed the digit for an emergency.

When a voice answered he said, "This is Colt Brannigan from the Floral Valley Ranch in Wyoming. I have to speak to Warden James tonight. She called me earlier today. I wasn't able to return it until now. This is urgent."

"Hold the line please."

"Thank you."

The blood was still surging through his veins when he heard a sound on the other end. "Mr. Brannigan? This is Warden James."

"I appreciate your coming to the phone. I know it's late, but this call is about one of the inmates, Geena Williams. She came to my ranch tonight looking for work, but she said she didn't talk to you about it."

"That's true. She must have seen your ad in the prison newspaper. When she left our facility this morning, she indicated she'd go to a women's shelter for the night."

"Why was she released when she's supposed to be serving a sixty-year sentence for murder?" Whatever answer she gave him wouldn't help, but he still had to know.

"She didn't tell you?"

Colt took a shuddering breath. "Tell me what?" he bit out.

"Yesterday morning I got word from the governor of South Dakota that Ms. Williams had been wrongfully imprisoned and the real killer has been caught."

"What?"

For the second time since coming in the den, Colt was on his feet, but for an entirely different reason. With the warden's explanation, he felt as though he'd just been freed from his own hellish prison after reading the hideous details on the Internet.

He hadn't been wrong about Geena. After what she'd been through, no wonder he saw that vulnerable look in her eyes.

"Ms Williams has been fully exonerated. She was given her certificate."

"Certificate?" he muttered, still in shock.

"It's a legal document—her passport to freedom, for want of a better word."

He realized it must have been in her backpack. "She spent a whole year in prison for nothing?" he blurted. After sustaining the shock, he was outraged for her.

"Yes. Hers was a very unusual case, very cruel. When I realized she had nowhere to go, I thought I might be able to help her find work and tried several places without success. After I learned that the position at your ranch had been filled, there was no point in telling her. I didn't want her to get discouraged."

Colt felt shame for having blown off the warden's phone call so easily. If he'd bothered to speak to her himself, he would have learned the truth about Geena and would have given her a chance to apply for the position. "She took the news well," he admitted. Hell— she'd been incredible about it!

"That sounds like Geena. I'm glad to hear she made it to your ranch safely and hope she finds work soon. She was a model prisoner in every sense of the word. It pains me that she was ever incarcerated."

His mouth had gone so dry, he could hardly talk. "That's all I needed to know. I'm more grateful to you than you know for coming to the phone. Goodnight, Warden."

"Goodnight, Mr. Brannigan."

He was so wired he knew there'd be no sleep for him tonight. After leaving a note in the kitchen that he'd be out on the range if an emergency cropped up, he headed for the back door.

Titus was right there with him and climbed in the truck before they took off. For the rest of the night he drove around thinking. He could hear his father's voice. *Everyone makes mistakes, Colt. This man deserves a second chance.*

But in Geena's case, she *hadn't* made a mistake!

Shocked when it got to be four-fifteen, he turned around and headed home with his mind made up about what he wanted to do. Before he parked the truck, his headlights shone on the big ponderosa further down the drive.

Her bike was gone.

* * *

At ten to six, Geena rode into the full-service gas station in Sundance. She was glad the dog hadn't heard her leave the ranch house. While Mr. Brannigan was still asleep, she'd been able to slip away unnoticed and get going. Her problem now was to wait it out until someone came to open the station so she could get a drink and use the restroom.

There were several piles of rubber tires stacked outside the bay doors. She propped her bike against one. Since no one was there, she pulled down two tires and sat on them while she rested against the pile. Once she'd covered herself with her space blanket, she was able to relax and plan out her day.

Her first destination would be the library. She'd scan the want ads online and find a job. If she ate only two meals a day and bought her food at the grocery store, she ought to stay afloat for a little while longer.

Tonight she'd sleep at the YWCA. She'd passed it yesterday on her way to the bike shop. In fact, en route to the library, she'd go over there and reserve a cot before they reached their quota for the day.

When it got to be seven-fifteen, she rolled off the tires and put them back, then walked her bike over to the restroom and rested it against the wall to wait. Pretty soon a man drove in and opened up the office. She said hello and followed him inside to get a soft drink. He went around and unlocked the restroom for her.

Once she'd used the facility, she opened the door, only to find her bike was gone! Geena had been in there only a minute. Frantic because of her loss, she raced around to the front, thinking she'd catch the culprit before he could get away.

"Relax, Geena."

At the sound of the deep, familiar voice, she swung around to face a clean-shaven Colt Brannigan standing at the side of the dark blue truck she'd seen parked outside the ranch house. His hard-boned features were shadowed beneath his black cowboy hat. This morning he was wearing a blue-and-green plaid shirt that covered his well-defined chest. Hip-hugging jeans molded to his powerful thighs.

Her thighs, in fact the whole length of her legs, wobbled just looking at him.

She'd never seen a sight like him and had the conviction she never would again, no matter how long she lived. When she'd left the ranch earlier, she'd determined to put all thoughts of him out of her mind. Geena had survived prison by shutting off her feelings. Surely she could do it again while she made a new life for herself, but this man was unforgettable.

"I was afraid someone would steal your bike, so I put it in the back of my truck for safekeeping."

Geena's heart was still racing too fast. She knew her upset over the stolen bike wasn't the only reason she couldn't seem to quell its tempo. Nervousness caused her to rub damp palms against her jeans-clad hips. "What are you doing here?"

He took a step toward her. "When I saw your bike was missing, I figured I'd find you in town. We have unfinished business this morning."

"Before I left, I put a thank-you note and a twenty-dollar bill on the kitchen table."

"I read it."

"I wish it were twenty times as much money. Last night I felt like a pampered princess. You could have no idea what it did for my spirits."

"I'm gratified to hear it." The way his gaze penetrated as he stared at her made her all fluttery inside. She folded her arms across her chest, not knowing how to contain her emotions.

"Most people wouldn't give a person like me the time of day. Last night at your hands I was treated to a taste of heaven. I won't forget. You're one in a million."

"You give me too much credit." The truth came out in a raspy voice. "Last night I couldn't restrain myself from looking on line to read the news articles about your imprisonment. They said you were supposed to be serving a sixty-year sentence for a capital one murder."

Geena eyed him calmly. "In that case I'm astounded you'd let a convicted killer stay through the night. Did you think I'd taken off with some of those authentic Sioux valuables and that's why you're here waiting to catch me with the goods? Or is it simply a question of morbid curiosity? You're welcome to search my backpack." She handed it to him.

His eyes narrowed before taking it. "If I'd thought you were untrustworthy, I would have driven you to town last night and dropped you off at the nearest shelter."

She had trouble breathing. "The housekeeping position hasn't been filled yet, has it?"

"No."

"I didn't think so. Thanks for being honest about that."

Colt didn't respond to her comment. Instead he opened her backpack and eventually drew out a brown envelope. She watched him reach inside and produce the certificate she'd read over and over again during her bus ride from Pierre, unable to believe she was free.

He studied it before his head reared. "Why didn't you show me this last night?"

"Because you told me the job had been filled. I didn't question it. You were incredibly kind to have brought me into the ranch house to sleep. In truth I was deathly tired last night."

"I noticed," he murmured.

"Before I fell asleep, I couldn't decide why you'd been so good to me. Was it out of an inborn sense of guilt and duty to one of your fellow creatures less fortunate than you? Or possibly even a modicum of faith in mankind? Whatever sentiment drove you, your mother would be proud of you. Now I'm afraid I have to get going to find a job."

He put everything back in her pack and handed it to her. "If you're still interested, I'm offering you the position of housekeeper. For a *temporary* period," he emphasized.

A small cry escaped her throat. Maybe she was hallucinating. "When did you make that decision?"

"After you went to bed last night, I called Warden James. Before I could ask her any questions, she told me you'd been exonerated and hoped you'd be able to find a job soon."

A tremor shook her body while she absorbed the revelation. "So—"

"So you see—" he interrupted her. "My mother wouldn't have been proud of me. In her mind, half a loaf doesn't cut it."

The blood pounded in her ears. "It cut it for me, so don't beat yourself. If I'd been in your shoes, I would have phoned the prison, too." She bit her lip. "Even if I'm innocent, why are you willing to take a chance on me?"

He put his hands on his hips, the ultimate male stance. "Besides your work ethic in prison which the warden praised, anyone who went through all you did yesterday to get the job deserves a chance. I came close to offering it to you before you went to bed, but the niggling thought that I'd seen or heard of you before propelled me to look on the internet first."

She paced a little, then stopped. "It was a hideous crime done to a dear friend. I spent thirteen months reliving the real killer's treachery to him. But I will always be a persona non grata in some people's eyes. Is that why your job offer is temporary? Because you know certain parties will refuse to believe the truth and it could cause trouble? Mind you, I'm not being ungrateful—just curious."

Lines bracketed his mouth. "To hell with what anyone else thinks. The position would be temporary to anyone I hired—a trial period, if you prefer. Both sides have to find out if the job is a good fit. You *did* say you only wanted it temporarily."

"Yes. What would you say if I work for you until the end of the summer? By then I have other plans and you'll have had time to find someone really suitable."

He studied her for a moment, then said, "End of summer it is. But when you've been with us a while, you might not want to stay that long, so your suggestion makes sense."

Mr. Brannigan was no one's fool. Being up front with him was the only honest thing to do. Then it wouldn't come as a surprise when she gave her notice to leave.

By then she ought to have a lead on the whereabouts of her brother's lover. And child. *If* it was his…

"Thank you for giving me this opportunity. How long have you been without a housekeeper?"

"A month. We've been hard hit by our previous housekeeper Mary White Bird's passing. You need to know she's been the only housekeeper on the ranch since my brothers and I were born."

"That long?"

He gave her a solemn nod. "Since her death, it's been hard even to contemplate someone else taking her place."

Geena's thoughts reeled. "She's the lovely Sioux woman in those pictures?"

"Yes," he said in what sounded like a reverent tone.

"You're right. No one could ever fill her shoes. I'm shocked that you'd let me sleep in her room among all her precious things. The tobacco bag is fabulous."

Emotion darkened his hazel eyes. "It belonged to her husband. I see you know your native American history."

Her throat swelled. "I learned a lot from Rupert." She eyed him directly. "Thank you for this wonderful opportunity. I realize Mary White Bird will never be forgotten, but for as long as I'm with you, I swear I'll work hard and not make you regret you hired me." Right now she felt she was the luckiest woman on the planet.

"In return I promise not to be too terrible a task-master, as my brothers continually remind me I am."

"Are you going to tell them I was in prison?" She hated the throb in her voice. They were standing close enough she could feel the warmth from his hard body.

"No. You've been exonerated for a crime you didn't commit, but that's up to you if you want to tell some-

one. As far as I'm concerned it's not information anyone needs to know."

She stole an extra breath. He was like a great bul-
wark in a storm. "You're a good man, Mr. Brannigan.
I'm so thankful for the job I could kiss your feet. But
not in front of the service-station attendant, who's been
watching us for some time."

The tautness in his expression relaxed. "I'll buy a
tank of gas, then we'll drive over to Tilly's and hash
out the details of your contract while we eat breakfast.
I'm in the mood for a big one. I don't know about you,
but I think better on a full stomach."

While he walked over to the gas pump, she climbed
in the cab of his Dodge Ram and held her backpack on
her lap. Through the back window she could see her
bike. She still couldn't believe he'd tracked her here in
order to offer her the housekeeping job. She was definitely being watched over.

In a few minutes they drove through the town of
1200-plus people to a spot he had to know well. Maybe
she was dreaming about the fabulous man who'd just
offered her a solid job on a ranch not more than seventy
miles from Rapid City. That's where she would begin
her investigation to recover her past.

The dreams just kept coming after they entered the
restaurant. Geena hadn't had waffles with strawberries
and whipped cream for over a year. With some slices of
ham added to the plate, she thought she'd never enjoyed
a meal so much. "You don't know how good this tastes."

"I can only imagine." He'd been watching her over
the rim of his coffee cup. "Are you up to some more
questions? Then you can fire away at me."

She sat back in the booth, already knowing the most

important thing about him. "Ask me anything you want, Mr. Brannigan."

"Call me Colt." When she nodded he said, "Where are you from?"

"I'll try to answer all your questions at once. I was born in Rapid City. My parents died young. My brother Todd and I were raised by our grandmother who lived on a fixed income and rented her home. I always did waitressing. After our grandmother died, I left for college in Laramie. Todd stayed at the house and worked laying pipeline."

"How did you manage financially when it was out-of-state tuition?"

"Through student loans and waiting on tables. I still owe $22,000. After graduation I went to work for a company in Rapid City called FossilMania."

"I've heard of it. What did you do there exactly?"

"We went out in teams in vans to find fossils. When we'd get to an area the owner felt contained dinosaur remains, we'd scour a certain section of land to begin a dig with our tools. I'm afraid that doesn't sound like a résumé for a housekeeper."

"Don't worry about it. Have you ever ridden a horse?"

"No."

"Then I'll teach you. Emergencies crop up from time to time. You'll be more useful in that kind of a situation if you can ride."

Geena wondered what circumstances he had in mind, but realized he was anxious to learn about her background. The questions she had for him could come later.

"In Rapid City I found an inexpensive basement apartment to rent from Rupert Brown."

She would have moved back to her grandmother's small house with Todd, but by then he had a girlfriend and she was living with him. Janice had disliked Geena on sight. She was so furtive, Geena knew the other woman had something to hide.

Her brother didn't have the best luck with women. Geena feared Janice was the wrong fit for him, but she'd never said anything to Todd because she loved her brother too much and didn't want to hurt him.

"Rupert and I shared an interest in artifacts and Native American memorabilia. Over the year I lived there we became good friends."

The next part sent a shudder through her. "One day when I came home from doing my field work, the police were there and arrested me for Rupert's murder. It had happened early in the morning and my fingerprints were all over the trowel I often used."

"You were framed!"

"Yes. A lot of his treasures had been stolen. Several of his irreplaceable books were found in my apartment along with my own small collection of fossils, all with my fingerprints."

"Someone had to know about your relationship with the victim."

"Definitely. It turned out to be a collector who'd come by his place when I'd been there with him. Various dealers interested in Western Americana often dropped in for a look at his things, hoping to get him to part with some of them, but his prices were too high. I think he did it purposely because he couldn't bear to part with anything. This angered the killer."

"If you were gone on long digs, the criminal had plenty of time to plant evidence in your apartment."

She nodded. "It gave me chills to think someone had been in there doing whatever. When I was put on trial, I couldn't afford an attorney, so a public defender was provided. I told him everything I could about the people who'd been to Rupert's apartment. I came up with a few names—any clues I could remember. But nothing came of it and the jury found me guilty."

"I don't know how you dealt with it," his voice grated.

"I think I was in shock the whole time. To be honest, I don't know why I didn't die on the spot. I wanted to. The thought of sixty years in that place, helpless to get out and do anything—"

A strange almost primitive sound came out of her new employer.

"Todd promised to find me a good attorney who could prove my innocence, but he didn't have any extra money. A month after I'd been put in prison, I got a message he'd been killed." Hot tears stung her eyelids.

"He was your only living relative?"

"Yes. I was notified through the warden's office by one of the executives at the pipeline company. He said there'd been an accident during an earth-removal incident, suffocating Todd and one of his co-workers. I was listed as the next of kin on his application. I swear the tragedy was more devastating to me than learning I'd be spending the rest of my life in prison."

Geena never knew what had happened to Janice. It was as if she'd vanished. More unconscionable, she'd never tried to get word to Geena about Todd. How anyone could be that heartless had almost destroyed her.

What made it so much worse was that the last time she'd ever spoken to Todd, he'd told her Janice was pregnant. He had hopes that a baby would settle Janice down and they could become a real family. Now that Todd was gone, Geena's only living relative might be the baby Janice would have delivered by now. But what if it wasn't Todd's?

While she was deep in her own tortured thoughts, lines had marred Colt's features until she almost didn't recognize him. "Who was the man from the pipeline?"

"A Mr. Phelps. He was decent enough to find out from me where my parents and grandparents were buried. I heard he made arrangements for Todd to be buried next to them at the cemetery."

Geena couldn't stop her voice from trembling and was unable to talk for a minute. One of the first things she wanted to do was go to the cemetery. After that she'd pay Mr. Phelps a visit and personally thank him for his kindness. She finally lifted her head. "But no more looking back. A miracle has happened."

She laid her napkin on the table. "Day before yesterday I was taken to the warden's office. She put me on the phone with the detective who'd been working on the investigation. He told me that some of Rupert's stolen artifacts had turned up. He found the real killer through new DNA evidence and arrested him. I almost did die right then. For *joy*."

She'd also talked to the public defender who'd represented her in court. He'd told her that within the month, the state would be reimbursing her some money for the time she'd been wrongfully incarcerated. The sum would be enough to help her carry out certain long-range plans. He gave her his number and told her to call him as soon as she had an address so he'd know where to send her the check.

When she looked up at Colt, his compassion-filled eyes were a sight she would never forget. "You've lived through something impossible for anyone else to comprehend. No platitudes could make up for the year you lost in there."

"That's true, but it's okay. It's over. You've offered me the job I wanted." It thrilled her to think that with the money she'd be receiving, she'd be able to pay Colt back for saving her life right now.

"Time will tell about that," he murmured.

She cleared her throat. "A minute ago you told me you used the word *temporary* in order for both sides to be ensured of a good fit, but I already know you're a good fit for me. That's because you were willing to be kind to me even after you knew I'd been in prison. There's a universe of difference between exoneration and a release for doing time."

Without his hat on, she thought he suddenly looked paler beneath the luxuriant wavy hair he wore medium-cropped. She couldn't decide if it was brown or black. Obviously it was a shade in between. "Are you all right? You look like you've seen a ghost," she murmured.

"Not even to be allowed to bury your own brother... You should never have spent one second in that prison," he whispered in a fierce tone without acknowledging her observation.

"But I'm free now, enjoying this delicious breakfast because of you!" she cried softly, still having to pinch herself. He represented a huge blessing in her life. Knowing she might have a niece or nephew out there filled her with the desire to work so hard for him, he would never complain.

In the process she'd try to find Janice and get a good

look at the baby. She'd know if it was Todd's. If it turned out to be his, then she hoped she could arrange for visits and keep their family connection alive. But there were still a lot of what-ifs....

Colt studied her as if trying to see into her soul. Geena could read his mind. She sensed that the guilty thoughts he'd entertained at the beginning, causing him to tell her the job had been filled, were going to weigh on him. She didn't want that for him.

"Stop running over yourself," she teased, warming to the side of him that had a strong social conscience. "When I showed up at your stable, you didn't tell me there was no room at the inn. That'll win you a lot of points in the next life. It's won them with me." The last came out in her husky voice.

CHAPTER THREE

"That's gratifying to hear." Emotion seemed to have deepened the green flecks in Colt's eyes. "If you're through eating, we'll drive over to the bank and set up an account for you. Which reminds me we haven't discussed your salary yet. What were you making at FossilMania?"

"Fifteen hundred a month."

"Did you have savings from that job?"

"A little. When Todd closed out my bank account for me, I told him to give it to the attorney he was going to hire, but he never got the chance." For all Geena knew, Janice had gone off with it, too.

Colt's lips thinned before he put some bills on the table for their meal. "For starting pay, how does twenty-five hundred a month sound? That includes room and board, two days a week off, a truck for your use and medical benefits."

She was staggered. "I think you know how that sounds." For one thing, she could start paying back her student loan. Any extra she could save would help her to make inquiries about Janice. "In fact, I doubt anyone else you hired would be offered as much."

"Being the housekeeper on the Floral Valley Ranch

covers a lot of territory. Mary made considerably more than that. In time you will, too, depending on how you like the work." Geena was certain she'd like the work, but she'd be working there only three months. That was their bargain. "Let's go."

They left Tilly's to walk to the bank located in the next block. By the time business had concluded, he'd arranged for an account to be opened in her name. The bank officer handed her a bank card and an envelope with a hundred dollars cash.

Colt took her elbow and ushered her out the doors. On the sidewalk he paused. "I've advanced you your first month's pay. You need a wardrobe and all the extras that go with it. You ought to be able to find what you want in the stores along here, so I'll leave you to get your shopping done. Bradford's is on the corner over there. I'll meet you out in front in say, two hours. If you need more time, we'll take it."

"I won't need two hours. You're too generous, Colt."

"When you've been with us a month, you'll realize you earned every penny of it and will be asking for a raise."

Some people had difficulty accepting gratitude. He seemed to fit in that category. "What am I supposed to wear during my work day?"

His eyes swept over her, but she couldn't read their expression. "Not a uniform. That's for sure."

"Thank you for that," she half laughed, putting a hand to her throat. His lips twitched in reaction. When he did that, her heart jumped.

"Put on whatever is comfortable."

She knew she looked pathetic in the hand-me-down clothes provided at the prison. Day before yesterday she'd been ecstatic to exchange the prison uniform for them. But today the knowledge that she could walk into a shop and pick out some new outfits made her so thrilled, she was close to being sick with excitement.

"I've never had the experience of buying a whole new wardrobe at once. You may regret you gave me this get-out-of-jail-free card. I might go hog wild."

He shoved his hat back on his dark head. "Frankly, ma'am, I hope you do."

With that remark, she knew she looked awful and didn't feel half as guilty while she spent the next couple of hours choosing clothes to wear, starting from the skin out. She went a little crazy on cosmetics and makeup. In the last store she tried on designer jeans and a white, form fitting Western shirt with pearl snaps and extended tails.

She loved the spread collar, not to mention the brown embroidery on the sleeves and yoke. The guy waiting on her brought out cowboy boots and a white cowboy hat to match. She'd never worn Western clothes like this in her life.

Geena put everything on and stood in front of the full-length mirror. Though she needed to gain ten pounds, the gleam in the clerk's eyes when he told her she looked fantastic made her feel better about herself and settled one matter for her. She would wear the whole outfit back home.

Yesterday she'd learned that the head of the Floral Valley Ranch was held in the highest regard in this part of Wyoming. If she was going to work for him, she needed to present herself in the best light.

Before she left the fitting room, she tossed her old clothes in the wastebasket. They'd been used by enough other women that she didn't feel guilty about discarding them. No doubt her new boss would be happy to know she'd gotten rid of them. To her relief the clerk, who'd been chatting her up, offered to help her out of the store with her all her bags.

She'd bought a lot of things, yet she knew he didn't normally offer to carry a client's purchases to the car for them. It had been a long time since she'd been around men. The attention from this nice-looking guy was fun and flattering. "Thanks for your help, Steve." It said Steve Wright on his name tag. "I really like my new clothes."

"On you, so do I. If you're going to be in town later, we could have dinner after I close up. How about it?"

"Afraid not" sounded a voice behind them with an underlying hint of steel. "She'll be at work."

Geena swung around to look at Colt. In the background she could see his truck double-parked. The piercing yellow-green of his eyes sent a tiny shiver down her spine. Was the transformation too much? She turned to the clerk. "Steve? This is my employer, Mr. Brannigan."

"Nice to meet you, sir."

While Colt nodded, Geena smiled at the clerk. "The next time I'm in town, I'll come by."

"Good. I'll be watching for you."

"Let me relieve you." Colt took care of all the bags before putting them in the back of the truck.

When the clerk went inside the store, Colt walked to the passenger side of the truck and opened the door for her. The boots made her a little taller, putting her on a better footing with him. Before she climbed in, she eyed him beneath the brim of her hat.

"You're probably upset about the purchase of this outfit. Tell me now if I've done something wrong. The only reason I decided to buy it was because you said I needed to learn how to horseback-ride. I want to look the part and fit in."

"What you buy is your business," he muttered.

"But there *is* a problem."

"There could be" came his cryptic answer. His gaze roved over her features visible beneath her cowboy hat. "It's not your fault," he added, as if it cost him to admit it.

Oh. Now she got it.

"You mean that I'm a woman?" It was absurd for Colt to think she was a femme fatale. She climbed in the truck so he could close the door. When he came around and got behind the wheel she turned to him. "He was just being a guy."

"I noticed."

"Look, Colt. I realize you employ a small army of men on your ranch. Sometimes a woman can cause trouble without meaning to. Todd told me stories about the problems with a few women who came out to see the men while they were laying pipe." That's where he'd met Janice. "But you have my promise that while I work for you, I'll keep everything professional. If there's a problem with any of them, I'll come to you immediately."

"I can't ask for more than that." There were invisible layers to this issue, but he wasn't willing to explain. They could be professional or personal. Maybe both. When she got to know him better, she'd find out.

He turned on the engine and joined the mainstream of traffic. "Before we head out of town, I'll take you over to the supermarket where we do our grocery shopping and introduce you to Bart, the manager. You'll be cooking for those of us in the ranch house. But he's worked with Mary and knows how to fill the lists for the food prepared by the cooks feeding the stockmen out on the range. The cooks come to the house to pick up from you once a week."

She averted her eyes. "You're right. There's a lot to learn. Who actually lives at the ranch house besides you and Hank?"

"Our mother and her caregiver, Ina. Then there's my brother Travis and his wife Lindsey. They live in the house close by, but eat their meals with us. She's pregnant and close to her delivery date. After the baby's here, they'll probably stay at the ranch house for a week, maybe more. Mary had been looking forward to taking care of the baby."

That meant Geena would be helping with its care. The idea excited her, but Colt had sounded far away just then. She had an idea that when they'd lost Mary, they'd lost a great deal more than a housekeeper. For Geena to think she could just step in and fill Mary's shoes was ludicrous, but she'd do her best not to disappoint him.

"Is Hank serious about the girl he brought home?"

"No. They've been friends since high school."

Geena smiled. "I don't think there is such a thing between a man and woman."

"No?"

"I saw the way she looked at him." Mandy was crazy about Hank. "But thanks for the information so I don't say something wrong. Tell me about my schedule."

"You work Monday through Friday. Your weekends are your own. Breakfast at seven, dinner at seven and lunch for our mother and Ina at one o'clock. The rest of us fix our own lunches if we come in. Most of the time we're out on the range and eat with the hands.

"When extended family and guests come for visits, they stay in the ranch house if there's room, or occupy a couple of the cabins nearby and join us for meals. Lindsey's mother will probably come and live at the house for some of the time. Occasionally business people fly in and stay over."

"I see."

"Mid morning Mary came to the post office in town to pick up the mail and left it on the desk in the den. Before we leave Sundance, I'll drive you over there to show you and give you a key to the box."

"I'll remember that." She glanced at him. "Tell me about your mother."

He grimaced. "She has full-fledged Alzheimer's and isn't going to get better."

"Oh no—how old is she?"

"Sixty."

"So young? I'm sorry, Colt. My grandmother's best friend had it toward the end." It was an awful disease. "Is Ina good to her?"

"Yes, but she needs help. Lately mother has been more restless and jumps up to walk around without warning. She needs more watching. After we leave the supermarket, I'm going to drop by the nursing service and see if I can't speed things up to get another caregiver to help spell off Ina."

Geena stirred in the seat. She was about to say she'd be glad to help out, but since she didn't know the full scope of her own responsibilities yet, she thought the better of it. As head of the family, Colt Brannigan had a lot of emotional worries to juggle along with running a big ranch. She was amazed at his capacity.

Bart turned out to be friendly to her and as respectful of Colt as the men she'd met at the Cattlemen's Store the other day. He went out of his way to assure her there would be help to load the truck when she came for large orders. All she had to do was pull around back to the docking area.

After kitchen duty for three hundred and fifty women in the prison, feeding six people twice a day didn't sound too daunting. Her biggest concern was to plan enjoyable, hearty meals for the men who were out in the saddle all day.

After they got back in the truck, Colt swung his head toward her. "Make that your second conquest of the day. It's a good thing he's happily married with four children."

How come you're not, Colt? Geena was dying to ask him that question, but he would have to tell her when he was good and ready. *If* he was ever ready.

"After being behind bars for a year with an all-female population, you have no idea how good it feels to be appreciated instead of being hated for being a woman. Right now I'm so thankful to be free and so thankful for my new job I can't even begin to tell you."

His gaze held hers for a moment. "I'm not unhappy about heading back to the ranch with a new housekeeper in tow. For the last month we've had to subsist on Hank's cooking. It hasn't been pretty."

She laughed before he started the engine and drove them to the medical center. Geena couldn't remember the last time she'd felt like laughing. Between her imprisonment and Todd's death, she'd thought there could be no state of happiness for her ever again. But sitting here in the cab waiting for Colt, she realized she'd been given a second chance to find it. All of it would be due to the striking, hard-muscled rancher entering the building and turning female heads left and right.

Gutted by the knowledge that Geena had been wrongfully imprisoned under the worst of circumstances, Colt could hardly concentrate on the nursing supervisor's words. To think she'd lived thirteen months behind bars for a crime she didn't commit! With the assurance that an aide would be available in another two weeks, he walked back outside and got in the truck. His cab had never smelled so fragrant.

Last night Colt had noticed the interest in Hank's eyes when he'd glimpsed Geena in the kitchen. The trouble was, that was before Colt had seen Geena turned out like *this*. In that outfit, she knocked every beautiful rodeo queen right out of the arena. He had no doubt Hank would fall all over himself trying to work his considerable charm on her. But Hank had enough problems. Colt didn't want him getting involved with Geena. Time would tell how well she fended him off.

The fact that she'd read Colt's mind after introducing him to the salesclerk a little while ago meant she understood some of his concerns. By her teens, men would have started coming on to her in droves. The way she'd handled the spiky-haired guy who'd called him sir, proved she knew how to deal with male attention.

Her assurance that the job was all that mattered to her right now gave him another reason to feel justified in hiring her, but unfortunately that promise wouldn't prevent his ranch hands from proving they were going to be the first to break through her defenses. And if one of them did, she planned to be gone by fall, so it didn't matter.

Naturally Geena's personal life in her free time was her own business. On that score Colt had no right to an opinion one way or the other. He glanced at her. "After we run by the post office, are there any more stops we need to make before leaving Sundance?"

An amused smile appeared on her face that already looked more relieved of tension. "Have you glanced out your rear window to see all the bags stashed back there?"

He chuckled. "I was thinking more along the lines of a rest stop or another meal."

"I think you're the one who's hungry again. How about we pull in to the Hungry Horse drive-in before going back to the ranch?" She could read his thoughts all right. "Do you know in prison I would dream about consuming a fresh limeade? I used to pay extra for half a dozen cherries to go with it. The combination of the two flavors can't be beaten. Crazy, huh?"

"Not crazy at all." He equated a fresh limeade with summer. Since his mother's illness, his father's death and Mary's passing, he'd forgotten what summer felt like. Geena's thoughts were attuned to his at unexpected moments.

What she didn't know was that he agreed with her about friendship between a man and a woman. It needed to exist alongside passion in a tight marriage, but outside of it, he didn't buy it any more than Geena did. His brother used Mandy, whose feelings for him were far from platonic.

To her credit she had a masterful way of covering

them up, but there would come a point when Mandy would wake up to the fact that his brother's interest lay in another woman and to waste any more time with him was futile.

With the mail collected, he headed for the drive-in. When it came their turn in the line of tourists, he ordered a steak burrito and two fresh limeades with additional cherries. Once they were on the road again he said, "I'm going to drive us back along the fire-break road. It'll circle around the ranch and take us up on some vista points so you can view the whole layout."

"Wonderful. How big is it?"

"Seventeen thousand acres. Eight thousand of them are deeded land."

"While I was riding my bike along here this morning, I yearned to get up on that mountain casting its long shadow over the valley. What's it called?"

"Inyan Kara. Some historians call it Hollow Mountain and others Stone-Made Mountain, but Mary said it comes from her language meaning 'mountain over mountain.'"

"I envy you having learned so much from her."

"The first Brannigan bought the property in 1872 and built the original part of the ranch house. We've survived five generations starting with the Sioux, then the U.S. Cavalry, followed by frontiersmen, pioneers, settlers, cowboys and outlaws."

She flashed him an infectious smile. "Oh, yes. The Sundance Kid. He and I have something in common, except I understand he was kept eighteen months in the Sundance jail before he was released and left the country. That's five months longer than yours truly out in Pierre's all-women prison."

Colt was glad she could be lighthearted about an experience that would have destroyed most people.

"One of my mother's ancestors was a pioneer from Scotland, but he didn't create an empire like your family has done," she volunteered. "What about your ancestry?"

"We're mostly English with a little Scotch-Irish thrown in."

"Our family has English blood too. How did your ranch get its name?"

Naturally the new housekeeper wanted to learn all she could. "General George Armstrong Custer rode through this area in early summer and saw the flowers in the high meadows. He called it Floral Valley and the name stuck."

"That's beautiful. In fact the beauty of this whole place takes my breath away."

She'd just put her finger on what was wrong with Colt. Since this morning when he'd found her at the gas station, he'd been in that condition and hadn't caught it yet. He drove them higher until they came to the first lookout where she could see the out buildings and the cattle grazing. Colt heard sounds of appreciation coming out of her before she started firing more questions. The woman had an inquisitive mind.

"We have a five-hundred-animal unit operation and bring in cattle on a rental basis over eighteen pastures. Sixteen of them have live water from the creeks and springs. For the other two, we've put in four wells and banks, along with earthen reservoirs."

She shook her head. "This is a huge enterprise."

"A lot goes on here, but it's manageable, although I'm a little short-staffed at the moment. Travis has had to stay close to Lindsey lately and Hank's broken leg has put him out of commission. Mac and the hands have been doing double duty."

"And you probably triple." This woman said all the right things. "Tell me what's beyond this vantage point."

"We have six hundred acres of wheat, and some other acreage of alfalfa and grass hay mix for use year round. We also have an income source from pasture lease, farmland crop-sharing and hunting fees."

"What do people hunt here?"

"Elk, deer, antelope and wild turkeys."

He heard a sigh. "Thank you for taking your time to give me a bird's-eye view of the ranch. I know there's a ton to learn and it will take me ages, but at least I can picture all this in my mind now. Otherwise I'd be like the proverbial deer in the headlights. It's an absolute paradise, Colt."

Not everyone felt that way if they weren't raised on a ranch. His ex-wife had come from San Francisco. Their two lifestyles had never mixed. He understood that. In Geena's case she'd be leaving in the fall, so it didn't matter if she took to the ranching life or not.

"In a few days when I have to inspect the herd, I'll take you with me so you can see the flowers Custer described. Now *that's* paradise."

"I'd love it," she murmured before he realized what had just come out of him. This was how you got in trouble. Geena was the new housekeeper. Her job was temporary. Period! She couldn't even ride a horse, and here he was planning an outing with her under the guise of work.

Yet hiring her had solved two problems. She needed a job and had provided a stopgap for him while he hunted for the right person to become another fixture on the ranch. Since Mary's passing a month ago, he hadn't had enough time to find that special person.

As for Geena, she had other plans. You didn't expect a woman like her to stay with the housekeeper position a long time, even if there were no contract. With her college degree she could make a whole new career for herself.

There were men out there—single, divorced, widowed—who were dying to link up with such an attractive woman. He'd already seen evidence of that today. She'd put prison behind her, and she expected to move on by the first snowfall. For the time being, the family needed Geena's services and she needed a few paychecks behind her before she left. But to his chagrin, the thought of her leaving didn't sit well with him, which was ridiculous.

He started the engine and drove them on a short cut through the pines to reach the house. Alice, one of the house cleaners, had parked her green pickup truck next to Hank's black one. Now would be as good a time as any for Geena to meet her.

After the truck was parked, she got down while he reached for the bags in the back. They entered the house and walked through to Mary's old room, except that from now on it would be known as Geena's.

Alice was in the bathroom scouring it, but stopped her work to see who'd entered the bedroom. "Hi, Colt."

"Hi, Alice. I'd like you to meet Mary's replacement." He put the bags down on the rug. "This is Geena Williams. She's from Rapid City, South Dakota. Geena? Alice White Eagle is a younger cousin of Mary's."

The pretty, fortyish mother of three was five feet one,

as Mary had been. Since Colt had known her, she'd kept her thoughts to herself, but clearly she was shocked by Mary's young replacement. The difference had to be astonishing to say the least. "Hello, Geena."

His new housekeeper removed her cowboy hat and put it on one of the two leather armchairs. Both women wore a braid. He'd discovered Geena looked sensational no matter how she did her hair.

"Hi, Alice. It's very nice to meet you." She shook the woman's hand. "I'm sorry Colt and I didn't come in sooner. I scoured that bathroom this morning. Now it has made extra work for you. Have you changed the sheets on the bed already?"

"Not yet."

"That's good because I found fresh sheets in the cupboard and changed them earlier."

"No problem." Alice's smile included Colt as she said it.

It might not be a problem for Alice, but Geena had known a different kind of hard work day in and day out for over a year. Colt hadn't realized she'd done those things to the room before creeping out of the house at dawn. She continued to surprise him in pleasant, elemental ways. It was as if she already knew the password to infiltrate the secret recesses of his psyche.

Geena glanced at the pictures on the dresser. "Those photos of your cousin are lovely, Alice. So is this room. You must miss her very much."

"Yes."

Colt's gaze flicked to Geena. "Alice is one of the three women who keep the ranch house spotless. We couldn't get along without them. They work a rotation. She comes in every third day. You'll meet Elaine tomorrow and Trish on Friday. They're usually here by eight-thirty and work till eleven, though Alice asked to start work later today. It'll interest you to know Alice's husband, Ben White Eagle, is our chief stockman."

Geena nodded. "I know that has to be hard work, but if you love animals it would be a pleasure."

Alice stared at her. "He's a man of the earth, like Colt."

"Who wouldn't love it in this beautiful place? Do you have children?"

"Three."

"What are their ages?"

"Thirteen, eleven and eight."

"How wonderful. I'd love to meet them. I hope you'll bring them sometime."

"Sometime I will. They're in school."

"Maybe bring them afterward for cookies and milk? My grandmother always made that for me."

Alice only smiled, but Colt knew that Geena wanting to include her children was a sure way to win her friendship. Geena had a way.

"Alice's family lives in one of the cabins further up the hillside, so occasionally you'll see them playing," he explained. "The other two women are married and live in Sundance with their families."

Geena nodded. "Have you worked here long, Alice?"

"Ten years."

"Then you're the person to come to if I have a question when Colt isn't available."

"Alice knows everything, but I'll go over the house-cleaning duties with you later," Colt interjected. "From then on you can meet with them if you have a special request or they need something from you."

"That sounds good to me. How about you, Alice?"

"It's good."

The soft-spoken woman couldn't help but be positively affected by Geena's friendliness. Had she always been easy to get along with? Or had she learned to deal with other women in prison and now had it down to an art form? Alice nodded in agreement and left the bedroom with her cleaning supplies.

"I'm sure you want to freshen up, then I'd like to introduce you to my mother. Will ten minutes give you enough time?"

"Plenty."

"Then I'll be by for you shortly."

CHAPTER FOUR

GEENA watched both of them leave the room. It excited her that Alice was also Lakota. Geena had a strong interest in native American history and would enjoy getting to know her better. No doubt it would be difficult for Alice to see someone else taking over the housekeeping duties that had been Mary's domain for several decades. Geena hoped in time they could become friends, but it wouldn't happen overnight.

Her mind flicked back to Colt. She went into the bathroom, only needing a minute before she was ready for him. Mrs. Brannigan might not recognize her loved ones any more, but she was Colt's mother, the one who wouldn't have approved of a half loaf.

There was a definite streak of cynicism running through her oldest son, though he kept it hidden for the most part. Like Achilles, the most handsome of all the heroes during the Trojan War, Colt appeared to be invulnerable in every part of his magnificent body *except* his heel. Achilles had died from a small wound received there.

Geena believed it was a woman who'd become Colt's only weakness. The fact that there was no mention of a woman in his life meant he still fought that weakness with all the breath he possessed. She'd sensed that much out under the ponderosa tree when his demeanor had sent out an aura that said *trespass at your own risk*.

She'd gotten the point instantly. Not that it was any of her concern. She was here to help keep order in Colt's house. Right now she wanted to look and be at her best for the woman who'd given birth to him. Anxious because she'd like to live up to all the things he expected of her, she expended some excess energy by going out into the hall while she waited.

The walls were lined with generations of family pictures. You name it and it was all there. She feasted her eyes on them. They dated from more than a hundred years ago to the present. Babies, little boys and girls, teenagers and adults. Parents, grandparents, great-grandparents. Some on horseback, rodeo shots, groups hiking, skiing, fishing.

The pictures of a younger, painfully handsome Colt winning prizes for steer-wrestling captured her attention. A young handsome Achilles all right. She found herself looking for every picture of him she could find from infancy to the age he was now. While she feasted her eyes on him with his family or alone, she heard footsteps in the hall and turned in that direction. It was his brother Hank.

"Well, hello again," he spoke first.

"Hi, Hank."

He moved toward her on his walking cast. His hair, a little overly long, had more brown in it than Colt's. Wearing jeans and a Western shirt, he was another good-looking Brannigan. She'd thought so last night. He had softer edges than Colt and was probably an inch shorter than his brother, who had to be six foot three.

"I didn't know you were still here." In his voice were all the questions she'd seen in his eyes last night, yet hadn't uttered. As his gaze swept over her, his pure green irises lit up in male appreciation. "It's the best news I've heard since the doc told me my leg was only broken in one place."

"Considering I can see you in the grouping of bull riders in these pictures, I suppose that *was* good news."

He let go with a hearty laugh. "Don't tell me you're a helper from the nursing service. I never saw one who looked like she was queen of the Sundance rodeo before."

That's what she looked like to him? How funny. Last night she'd resembled a bag lady. Geena didn't know what Colt would want her to say, but since he hadn't arrived yet, all she could do was be honest. "I came here to apply for the housekeeping position."

The charming flirt looked blown away. "You've got to be kidding! Who let you in the house?"

"Your brother."

His brows lifted. "How come you're still here?"

With that one question, Hank had just told her a mouthful about the hard inner facing of his older brother, who would never have hired her under normal circumstances. But there'd been nothing normal about her meeting with Colt. What Hank didn't realize was that his brother was suffering from a surfeit of guilt about her. In order to assuage it, he'd hired her for a *temporary* period.

No one knew that better than she did. It was just as well, because she was on a mission to find Todd's girlfriend, wherever it took her. "He decided to try me out on a probationary basis."

Looking stunned, Hank muttered something unintelligible under his breath.

"I'm very happy about it and hope your family will be too." She was more thankful than ever for the new clothes she was wearing as well as the other things she'd bought. Besides lingerie she now had jeans, tops, a few skirts and blouses, some sandals and a new purse and wallet. All things she'd once taken for granted, but prison had changed her perspective and priorities.

"Where are you from?"

"Rapid City."

After a long pause he said, "Since you're new to Wyoming, keep Saturday night open and I'll show you around Sundance. We'll do some line-dancing. How does that sound?"

"It sounds fun and I'm flattered," she said without having to think about it. "But whenever I'm employed, I have rules. No socializing within the company. In the case of the Brannigans, no fraternizing with the family or those employed on the Floral Valley Ranch. Besides, you can't dance until that cast comes off."

The playfulness left his eyes. "Did Colt tell you to say that?"

"I've been a working girl for a long time, Hank. I set my own rules." She'd learned how to protect herself in prison in order to survive.

He studied her for a minute, clearly stymied. "What are you doing out here in the hall alone?"

"Your brother should be along any second. He's taking me to meet your mother."

"He might be a while. When I passed him, he was on the phone with Sheila making his plans for the weekend. Come with me. Ina's probably taken Mom outside."

Had she been completely wrong about Colt? Silly how her heart pounded harder because she thought this Sheila could be someone important to him. *It's none of your business, Geena.* It couldn't be!

She followed Hank to the master bedroom. In truth it was an apartment with a fireplace and a den. She loved the vaulted ceiling and Western motif. The double doors were open onto a covered veranda.

Geena picked out their slim mother immediately. She was dressed in jeans and a blouse and was probably five feet four. Instead of boots, she wore sneakers and sat on a covered swing with her hands on her knees, as if she was getting ready to stand up and go. She resembled Hank in coloring, but there were sprinklings of silver in her short brown hair and some of the facial features were reminiscent of Colt's.

"Hi, Mom." Hank bent down to kiss her cheek. "Someone's come to see you. Laura Brannigan, meet Geena Williams, our new housekeeper." Eyes more brown than hazel stared at Geena without animation. There was no recognition before Hank finished the introductions. "Geena, meet her caregiver Ina Maynes."

"How do you do?" They shook hands. Ina was a bigger woman with blond hair, probably in her early fifties. She sat on a chair next to the swing. On the coffee table were a lot of books and magazines.

"How's she been doing since lunch?" he asked Ina.

"The same. Restless. She roamed the house this afternoon."

"That medicine the doctor prescribed should start to work by morning."

Geena glanced at Hank. "What kind does she take?"

"It's a new prescription for her anxiety."

Their mother continued to use her right foot to push off.

"Here you all are." Colt had come out on the veranda. Geena wished her body didn't quicken at the sound of his deep voice. His gaze flicked to her. "I see you've met mother and Ina."

"Yes. Hank caught me in the hall looking at the pictures. We're just getting acquainted."

"That's good." He turned to Ina. "Why don't you take a break until dinner? Geena and I will go for a walk with her."

"Thanks. I've got a letter to write."

Somehow Geena needed to keep reminding herself there was nothing personal in Colt's suggestion. For him it was vital she get to know the inner workings of the family so life on the ranch could get back to some kind of normal for them.

He reached for his mother's hand and helped her up from the swing. Still holding it, he waited until she'd stepped to the grass before he let go. Geena walked on her other side, enjoying the lush greenery surrounding the house.

"We'll head for the stream in the distance. It's one of our favorite places. When we were little tykes, she'd make picnics and teach us boys how to fish there, didn't you, Mom?"

Geena fought the tears smarting her eyelids as she noticed Laura make a beeline for the cottonwood trees lining the water's edge. All the memories of her life were locked up inside, but she seemed to know instinctively where she wanted to go. Every so often Geena eyed Colt with a covert glance. This had to be so hard for him and his brothers. She was touched by their love and devotion.

When they reached the rippling brook, his mother stood there quietly and stared. "What are the things she used to like?"

Colt angled his head toward her. "She loved to cook and garden. Now that she's at this stage, I have no idea. All we do is try to replicate what she used to enjoy—play her favorite music and read to her from the books she loved. She likes walks."

"What about horseback-riding?" His dark brows lifted in surprise. "From the pictures, she looked like an accomplished rider."

"She was a top barrel racer from her late teens on. That's how she and Dad met. He was a bull rider."

"That sounds like a magical beginning for them. Is there a reason she can't still ride if it's with supervision?"

He looked taken aback by her question. "I don't know. It's food for thought." She saw the love in his eyes as he looked at his mother through his black lashes. "Speaking of food, I bet you're hungry, Mom. Hank ought to have dinner ready for us pretty soon. Let's start back."

Colt took her hand and the three of them headed for the house. The mention of his mother's interests had Geena's mind racing with an idea. She couldn't wait to try it out once she was used to her official duties.

He took them around the house to the front drive where they could enter through the front door. This way he gave Geena a tour of the rustically decorated main floor. A marvelous hand-carved staircase rose from the center of the massive foyer. On the right it was flanked by a spacious living room, all vaulted with timbers. Beyond it lay a family room with a stone fireplace and furniture upholstered in red-and-green plaid.

On the left of the main hall was a dining room with a carved oak table and matching hutch. She counted twelve chairs. Down one hall she saw a study with display cases filled with trophies of all kinds and a large rack of antlers over the lintel. The other hall led to the big kitchen and another hall where Geena would be living.

"Lindsey's not feeling well, so I'm going to run dinner up to them," Hank announced when they entered the kitchen. The food was on the table ready to be served.

"I'll do it," Colt offered. "Be right back."

"I don't mind."

"With your leg in a cast, you'd have to walk. I can drive there in two seconds." She heard that same voice of authority she'd heard him use with the salesclerk. Already she was learning that Colt was by nature a fixer and took it upon himself to help everyone. Again she was impressed by that caring.

Hank gave up the argument but Geena noticed he wasn't happy about it. When Colt's logic couldn't be faulted, she wondered why it seemed so important to Hank. By now Ina had joined them at the table.

Geena started eating. "This spaghetti's delicious." He'd served canned fruit cocktail and store-bought bread.

"Thanks." He was still upset. "I can cook three things and the family's sick of them all."

Ina chuckled. "That's not true, Hank. We've enjoyed your meals." She helped Laura eat while she ate. Colt's mother appeared to have a good appetite and didn't turn away any food. She was such a lovely woman. Too young for this. Todd had been too young to die. Life could be cruel.

Hank's eyes focused on Geena. "I hope you can cook because I'm living for tomorrow when I don't have to eat any more of my…stuff." He'd almost said something else, reminding her of her brother Todd when he'd been in a grumpy mood. Hank appeared to be around thirty years of age, the same as Todd would be now if he were alive. She missed her brother so much, she still felt deep pain when she thought of him.

"I promise I won't make spaghetti for a month."

His dour expression didn't change. "That's a comforting thought." Hank had a big chip on his shoulder. She suspected her negative response to his invitation to go dancing hadn't helped his mood this evening.

"I would imagine you'll feel a lot better once that cast comes off. How much longer for you?"

"Next Monday. It's been a royal pain."

She was about to ask him how he'd broken it when Colt came back in the kitchen. He shot her a glance as he sat down at his place. "Have you been talking about me again?"

Ina chuckled, but Hank countered with another question. "What's wrong with Lindsey?"

"She's been having some contractions, but Travis said the doctor didn't think they'd last. They've stopped for now." His spaghetti disappeared fast. Geena would have to fix a lot of food to keep him satisfied.

Hank didn't move a muscle, but she could tell he was disturbed about something. Colt on the other hand went on eating as if nothing in the world could possibly be wrong. On impulse she got up from the table.

"I'm going to get myself some more coffee. Anyone else want some?"

"You can fill mine again," Colt answered.

She poured him another cup, realizing this was going to be her job from now on. It felt good to be useful again, especially in this household with all its dynamics and tensions, the kind that existed in a normal home. She'd missed the feeling of family.

It hadn't been the same after Todd had brought Janice home to live. Geena had wanted her brother to find the right woman and get married. She thought about the way Janice treated him and shuddered when she tried to imagine Janice with a baby. If Janice couldn't remain true to one man, the baby would suffer from the instability.

Geena had to stop thinking that way and sat down to finish her fresh cup of coffee. When she was through, she'd come to a decision and got to her feet once more. After picking up her plate, she walked around the table to remove Hank's, hoping to improve his cranky disposition.

"I take it you've been chief cook and bottle washer around here for a month, Hank, but no longer. Naturally I don't know where everything goes yet, but if I do the dishes myself, I'll find out. By tomorrow morning I'll be ready to tackle the meals."

The frown on his face turned to one of surprise before his chair shot back. Despite his cast, he stood up in a hurry. "Glory hallelujah!" was all he said before disappearing down the hall.

Ina took her cue and got up to walk Laura back to her room. That left Colt who started clearing the rest of the table. Even though the kitchen was roomy, his tall, powerful body seemed to fill it. He eyed Geena. "Two pairs of hands make the work go faster. Don't you agree? While we work, ask me all the questions you want."

She took him up on his offer, loving the cozy, domestic feeling now that they were alone. Around him her heart rate ran at a higher speed and there wasn't a thing she could do about it.

"Where's Titus?"

"He's sleeping up at Mac's place tonight. Mac Saunders is the ranch foreman. I'll introduce you to him and his wife, Leah, when it's convenient. Their family adopted Titus a long time ago. Everyone misses Dad and the dog is a reminder."

"That's so sweet. What kind of food do you feed him?"

"It's right here." He opened one of the cupboards and showed her everything, including his doggie treats.

"What about your mother? Does she require a special diet?"

"No. The doctor only said her meals should be well-balanced."

"Everyone needs that."

"We kind of fell down in that department this last month. As you noticed, Hank's been a limping time bomb." He flashed her a grin before emptying the dishwasher. She hadn't seen that particular look before. It made him too appealing.

While she loaded it, she watched where he put the clean dishes and utensils. After wiping off the counter, she cleaned the oven top. Colt took care of the table. Before she knew it they were done.

"Follow me to the walk-in pantry. The laundry room

is through that other door on the right." She did his bidding, marveling at the amount of food storage. The pantry was really another room.

"The big freezer is out in the mudroom. You'll find all the cuts of beef, pork and lamb you want. Everything's labeled. The freezer side of this fridge has chicken, ham, bacon, sausage. The rest is usually full of vegetables, fruits, salad, eggs, milk, cheese, yeast. The flour and sugar are kept in the bins on the right side of the dishwasher."

He'd mentioned all those items for a reason and Geena tried not to laugh out loud. "Thank you for the grand tour." She had an idea they hadn't eaten like they used to since Hank had taken over in the kitchen. Colt had put his point across big-time. Now it was up to her to produce those meals he was definitely salivating about. No worries there. Her grandmother had been a great cook and Geena had learned everything from her.

"Okay," he said, lounging against the counter with his strong arms crossed. "Ask me the question that's been bothering you since we came into the kitchen with mother."

The man had radar. "I don't know what you mean."

"That's the first lie you've told me since we met."

"What I'm thinking or wondering while I get to know your family is private and not important, Colt."

"It is to me. Out with it."

"This is about Hank," Geena whispered.

"I knew it. He needs to apologize for his rudeness. I'll talk to him. Let's go for a ride where we can be private. You won't need your purse unless you want it."

Alone with Colt. Excitement chased through her like the cool breeze she'd felt at the service station when she'd heard his voice and had discovered he'd followed her.

They left out the back door. He walked her past the other trucks and cars to a smaller, two-door white Ford pickup. "This is yours from here on out. The last person to drive it was Mary, but she didn't have long legs like yours." While she quivered from his personal comment, he opened the driver's side for her. "Go ahead and get in so you can adjust the seat the way you want."

Her arm accidentally brushed against his shoulder as she climbed in. It sent arcs of electricity through her nervous system. Her body was still reacting to his touch and made her clumsy as she tried several times to position the seat at the proper distance. He'd opened the door on the other side to watch. His action didn't help.

Finally she got it right. "There." As soon as she said the word, his masculine frame climbed in next to her. She couldn't help but be aware of his long, rock-hard legs. "Did you ever drive around in this with Mary?"

"No."

"I didn't think so."

They both chuckled before he handed her the truck keys on a ring. "Go ahead and take us up the road."

She started the engine. The tank was three-quarters full. "It's been a long time for me."

He slanted her a glance. "You rode your bike all those miles, so I don't see a problem."

The automatic transmission made it easy. After backing out, she headed up the hillside past the outbuildings. He pointed out Travis's place and Ben and Alice's cabin. Farther on, Mac and Leah's house. With him giving her directions, they reached another area of the property featuring open rolling grasslands.

"I dreamed about times like this in prison. You have no idea what it means to be free." Her voice shook. "I'm sorry if I talk about it so much. I'll try to stop."

His profile took on a chiseled cast in the semi-darkness. "Three nights ago you were still behind bars. Like a returning war vet, you'll always have that memory with you. But hopefully in time, the experience won't traumatize you."

"Are you speaking from personal experience?"

"Not exactly. I have a cousin, Robert, who's my age and lives in Casper, Wyoming. He was in the military, but he hasn't been the same since he got home last year. Though he's in therapy and doing better, he still has occasional flashbacks and flies up to the ranch for a few days every so often to talk to me."

"The poor thing. PTSD?"

"Yes."

"There was a woman in my cell block who'd served in Iraq. When she got back, she torched her stepfather's warehouse because he beat up her mother. She didn't know he was inside. His death sent her to prison. Sometimes at night we'd hear her screams and have to listen to things that made my skin crawl. She needs help."

Colt shot her another glance. "After what you've been through, you could benefit from some professional therapy yourself."

"Warden James told me the same thing," she admitted.

"The insurance I pay for you would cover a psychiatrist. Robert's is one of the best around."

"But if he's in Casper, that's pretty far away."

"No problem. I do regular business there with my uncle and will fly you in our Cessna from Taylor Field.

If you'd like, I'll leave the doctor's name and phone number for you on the kitchen counter by the phone."

Panic enveloped her because she sensed Colt was already worried about his new housekeeper. Part of her hoped he cared for her in a more personal way, but maybe she was deceiving herself. After all, that is what he did: he cared for people and took care of them.

It was natural for him to be concerned over everyone on the ranch. He carried their problems on his back. Since she needed this job desperately, she'd better go along with his suggestion. Not that she'd find herself out of work if she didn't. He wasn't like that. But she wanted harmony between them.

"Thank you." What else could she say? Deep down, she knew she needed help from an outside source and was grateful. "If you'll do that, I'll make an appointment."

"Good." He sounded relieved. "At the next rise, there's a lookout where you can pull to a stop."

She drove a little further till she came to it. Evening had fallen. The surroundings of rough hills with steep ravines beyond them was surreal. Geena shut off the engine and got out of the cab. He joined her as they took in the vista.

"After his release, the Sundance Kid was a fool to leave Wyoming," she said. "He could have redeemed his life by starting all over again right here, on a spread just like yours."

A chuckle escaped Colt's lips before he sobered. "It looks beautiful, but it has its headaches. Tell me what happened with Hank today."

Colt was a natural-born leader who took on the mantle of the ranch and everyone's problems without thinking about it. He really was a breed apart from other men, and he already had a tentacle hold on her heart.

CHAPTER FIVE

"HE asked me to go dancing on Saturday night," she answered without pretending to misunderstand. Colt knew it had to be something like that. "Naturally I turned him down."

"On what grounds?"

"That I have a rule never to combine the personal side of my life with business. I thought he'd handled the rejection just fine, but later at dinner he seemed upset."

"No man likes to be turned down, but Hank had more than your rejection on his mind, trust me." He cocked his head, feeling very protective of her. "I'll have a talk with him." His brother was a bit of a player.

"Maybe you shouldn't. I don't want to hurt his feelings."

Her caring stirred Colt's emotions. "Anything else you'd like to ask me?"

"I wondered how he broke his leg in the first place."

"At the rodeo in Laramie. The bull stomped on him before he could roll out from under him."

"Oh no— Is Hank a champion?"

Colt nodded. "He's won a lot of prize money. This year he was hoping to win the world championship in Las Vegas coming up in December, but this broken leg has cost him a lot in practice time. He could go for it next year, but he's not getting any younger. That's a demon he can't fight."

"What will happen if he doesn't compete any more this year?"

"He'll keep doing his work here on the ranch."

"That explains a lot of his pent-up frustration." She flicked him another glance. "In the hall I saw pictures of you steer-wrestling. When did you stop competing?"

He hadn't expected that, but she deserved an answer. "After I got married. By the time we were divorced, I had too many ranch responsibilities to consider going back to competition."

"I see."

Colt waited for the inevitable fallout questions, but they never came. She wasn't like any woman he'd known before. She'd gotten under his skin, all right. If he felt this way right now, how would he handle her leaving at the end of the summer? Before more time passed, he intended to ask her about her future plans.

"Before we go back, there's something else you should know. Lindsey's going to have that baby any minute. She's very good-looking and high maintenance. So's her mother. After she gets out of the hospital, don't let either of them order you around."

"Being the new inmate on the block, I learned the hard way about bullying. The trick is not to let them get away with it the first time." Geena's smile revealed a hint of toughness. She had grit, all right.

"That goes for headstrong animals, too."

"Thanks for talking to me, Colt. I think I'm ready to face tomorrow."

He shifted his weight. "One more reality check. Are you feeling overwhelmed yet?"

She took her time before answering. "I'd be lying if I didn't tell you I'm nervous that I won't be able to live up to your expectations. But having said that, you don't know how nice it is to be around a real family where I can try to help make things easier. Your load is huge. I could ask you the same question about feeling overwhelmed."

"I admit sometimes I am. When everyone needs you at once, it can be a little suffocating, but that feeling passes. We were talking about your problems." She had the ability to draw him out when he least expected it.

"In prison I learned about work. It's the great panacea."

Work had always been his panacea, but lately he'd found out it wasn't nearly enough. That appeared to be Geena's fault. Fighting her charisma was like battling a force of nature.

"If there's any advice I can give you as your employer, treat the ranch house as your own home. Make it yours."

"Thank you."

"If you want to change the decor in Mary's old room, you have my permission to do whatever you want with it."

"I couldn't!" she emoted. "It's like living inside a fabulous museum. I love it."

"You'd make her happy if she heard that. The entertainment center is in your bedroom armoire but keep in mind we have a family room you saw off the living room. It's there for your use any time. And something else." He pulled a cell phone out of his pocket. "I bought you this and a laptop today while you were shopping."

She took it from him. Though brief, he felt her touch like a white-hot brand. "You've thought of everything!"

"We need to be able to keep in touch. I've programmed my cell phone number on two, and put your number in my phone. You can phone long distance or out of the country. Later you can program in the other phone numbers you want.

"I also loaded the laptop and left it in your room. Look through it when you have time. If you have problems navigating, I'll help you. It contains all the information you need on the staff. Phone numbers, addresses. That includes the hands and stockmen. Emergency numbers.

"As for the house inventory, once you have a grasp, it'll make a difference in what supplies you order and how much will be needed at one time. You're welcome to use the computer in the den too."

"All I do is say thank you." She put the phone in her front pocket. "Now there's something I have to say to you."

"That sounds serious."

"It is. Don't ever hold back if you've discovered I've done something wrong or overstepped my bounds or dealt with something in a way that made things worse. The only way I can learn is for you to tell me straight up, Colt. No lies, no tiptoeing around the truth to spare hurt feelings."

Her earnestness brought out more of her natural beauty. "In other words, no quarter asked."

"None. I'm a big girl going on twenty-eight. I grew up after I was put in prison."

Prison was the word that came up in her conversation more than any other. Colt decided he was the one who needed therapy if he was going to be able to handle it. "Then I would say we understand each other."

"Yes."

She beat him back to the truck and started the engine. They returned to the ranch house while another amazing full moon started its ascent. She poked her head out the window. "Can you believe we actually went up there?"

"One of our hands thinks it was a hoax."

"Several inmates were convinced it was a conspiracy, too. To be honest, I really don't care what they believe. How could anyone care on a night like this? Umm. Fresh mountain air. There's nothing like it."

"I agree with you."

"I know one thing. I'll never take anything for granted again."

Almost to the house, his cell phone rang. He checked the caller ID and picked up. "Hank?"

"Travis left me a message that Lindsey's water broke. The doctor told him to drive her to the hospital."

Colt was afraid he knew why his brother sounded so anxious. "This is what we've all been waiting for."

"Where are you? Haven't you checked your messages?"

For once Colt had been too involved in his conversation with Geena to think about anything else. "I was busy."

"Shouldn't we do something?"

"Not until Travis asks us. I'll see you in a few minutes."

After he clicked off Geena said, "I take it the baby is coming. Is it a boy or a girl?"

"A girl."

"You're going to be an uncle before you know it. That's exciting."

It should be. But having both his brothers in love with the same woman clouded the picture for Colt. "Now that we're back, you go to bed, Geena. It's been a long day. I'll see you in the morning."

"Thank you for giving me a new start. I'll always be indebted to you." She jumped down from the truck and hurried into the house without drawing out their conversation. Was she a little spooked by Colt? He'd gotten the impression she was a very private person, but maybe he made her nervous. By the time he walked through the back door, she'd disappeared.

He moved through the house to check on his mother. She was in bed asleep. All was quiet from Ina's room. After locking up and turning out lights, Colt climbed the stairs. Hank met him at the top and followed him into his bedroom.

"Where in the hell have you been?"

"I gave Mary's truck to Geena. She drove us a ways while she got used to it."

"That's quite a transformation from the woman I met in the kitchen last night. What's the story on her? I didn't see a car."

"She didn't have one. Geena arrived on her bike to interview for the position." Straight from prison.

"She's a biker?"

"Not in the sense you mean. She has a road bike. I put it inside the storage shed for safekeeping."

"So where did she sleep last night?"

Colt was getting tired of answering his questions. "In Mary's old room."

"You're kidding! You mean you hired her on the spot?"

No, but for reasons he still hadn't examined, he hadn't want to see her leave. "Not until today. With Ina occupying the guest room on the main floor, I had to put her somewhere last night." Certainly not upstairs in the other guest room across from Hank's bedroom.

His brother might take it on himself to get more acquainted with her and start asking questions. Geena would rather no one knew about her time in prison. Colt didn't want his brother making her uncomfortable.

"Can she even cook?"

Geena's looks had knocked his brother sideways. Obviously, so had her rejection. But his brother was so mixed up emotionally, it was hard to read him. "I guess we'll find out tomorrow. At least you're off the hook. She's temporary until fall. By then I'll find a woman like Mary to replace her."

"Fat chance."

Colt agreed, yet he had to honor the contract he'd made with Geena. That meant he needed to put out more feelers for a permanent housekeeper, but the idea of her leaving was growing unacceptable to him.

"Let's just be thankful that with the baby coming, someone will be here to help out. A word of warning, Hank. Let's respect her boundaries, hmm?"

His brother sighed. "I'm going to have to, since she turned me down for a date."

Good. The resignation in Hank's voice told him all he needed to know. "That makes for less complications around here. Go to bed, Hank. We'll hear from Travis

before long. I don't know about you, but I'm whacked."
Except that Colt knew he'd have another sleepless night.

When the alarm clock went off at five-thirty, Geena
jumped out of bed to get ready for her first day of work.
She'd showered last night, so all she had to do was put
on a fresh pair of jeans and a plum-colored cotton crew
neck sweater with short sleeves. While she rebraided
her hair and put it on top of her head, she wondered if
the baby had been born yet.

After applying a pink lipgloss, she slipped on sandals
and hurried through the house to the mudroom. Tonight
she would serve leg of lamb with all the trimmings.

Once she'd taken it out of the freezer and put it aside
in the kitchen to thaw, she made coffee, then got bacon
and sausage from the fridge. They'd taste good with
scrambled eggs. For an added treat, she made milk
gravy and baking powder biscuits. She'd forgotten how
much fun it was to cook. Her grandmother's recipes
were the best.

By five to seven, everything was ready and she'd
poured the orange juice. As she added two kinds of jam
to the table, her employer entered the kitchen in a tan
Western shirt and jeans. He could have no idea how his
incomparable masculinity affected the opposite sex.

"Good morning, Geena. Something in here smells
fabulous."

He smelled marvelous himself. "I hope it tastes as
good." Colt was so striking, she busied herself pouring
him some coffee at the place where he'd sat last night.
"Do I take it you have a new niece?"

Before he sat down, his hazel gaze appraised her so
thoroughly, she could hardly breathe. "Not yet, but I

suspect it won't be long now. After breakfast Hank and I will drive to Sundance and see how things are going. By the way, I spoke to Hank last night. He gets it."

Geena's heart warmed to him even more for being concerned. "Thank you for telling me." While he drained his glass of juice, she went over to the stove and made up a plate for him. "Do you like milk gravy on your biscuits?"

"I like everything. Bring it on."

"You sound like my brother Todd."

"How old was he when he died?"

"I'd say Hank's age."

"Were you close?"

"Very." Until Janice moved in with him. She was probably living with another guy by now. And what about the baby? Was it even alive?

Stifling another shudder, she brought his plate over and set it in front of him. "Before I serve anyone else, does anyone in the house have allergies I should know about? Or foods they truly don't like? Especially your mom?"

He ate two sausage links before he flashed her a sideward glance. "Not to my knowledge, but I appreciate you asking. Won't you join me?"

"Not yet. I'm waiting for everyone to come." In truth she derived pure pleasure from watching him eat while she propped herself against the counter to drink her coffee. Anticipating his desire for more biscuits, she took a plate of them to the table. In a minute they disappeared.

Soon a guest she hadn't thought of came flying into the kitchen. He plopped his head on Colt's leg.

"Hey, Titus." He rubbed his fur. "Mac must have

brought you home." His presence reminded Geena to put out dog food for him.

After feeding the dog a sausage, Colt got up from the chair and left and, before she knew it, he came back into the kitchen with a dark-blond man who had to be in his mid forties. "Mac Saunders? Meet Geena Williams, our new housekeeper."

Mac removed his cowboy hat and shook her hand. "Pleased to make your acquaintance, ma'am."

"Sit down and have breakfast with us," Colt insisted. "These biscuits and milk gravy are to die for." Colt sounded like he'd meant it.

"Yeah?" the foreman grinned. His blue eyes lingered on Geena before he complied.

"Let me take your hat." She put it over on one of the other counters before she served him a plate.

"Yup," he said a minute later. "I think I just died and went to heaven."

Colt eyed her briefly. "Did you hear that, Geena?"

"If it's food, men love it," she teased.

"*This* is food—" Mac blurted with such enthusiasm it warmed her heart. While the two men discussed the day's work schedule, she heard other voices.

Hank came in, making record time with that cast on his leg. He was followed by Ina and their mother. Geena was kept busy serving everyone. She buttered a hot biscuit for Laura and put blackberry jam on it.

"No word from Travis yet?" Ina inquired. Colt shook his head. "A first baby usually takes a long time."

"We're going to see him after we eat," Hank muttered. The other two men continued to talk business. Geena poured everyone a second cup of coffee and kept the food coming. Before long a restless Hank got up from the table. "Coming, Colt?"

"As soon as I've had one more of Geena's biscuits. I think I've eaten half a dozen."

Mac laughed. "With food like this, you're going to gain weight fast. Much obliged, Geena." He got up and walked over to the counter for his hat.

Hank wheeled around and left the kitchen in a temper Geena could feel. Colt eyed her briefly before he got to his feet. Though Colt had explained some of Hank's problems to do with his broken leg and his rodeo career, he hadn't told her everything. Nor had Colt explained about his own wife or his marriage. "See you later."

After the men left, Ina stood up. "That was a delicious meal, Geena."

"Thank you. I'm glad to see Laura enjoyed it too."

"She surely did."

"Colt said you eat lunch at one o'clock."

"Yes, but after all this, I'm not sure we'll be hungry. Don't go to a lot of trouble. Make something light. See you later."

Once they'd gone, Geena put more food and water out for Titus, then cleared the table and did the dishes. Before long she heard a female voice call out hello. It turned out to be Elaine Ruff, one of the house cleaners coming into in the kitchen. Evidently all three women had keys. They chatted for a few minutes. Elaine informed Geena that today was the day she washed windows.

Geena told her to go about her usual business, then she changed clothes and drove into town. She needed to pick up the mail. After that she renewed her driver's license and then bought produce. Ina had said she wanted something light for lunch so Geena decided to pick up some fresh crab for a salad.

Before she started back to the ranch, she made one more quick stop near the town center.

Colt entered the back of the house with no time to spare before dinner. He'd planned it this way on purpose. After leaving the hospital at eleven that morning, he'd seen the white truck parked in front of the police station on his way out of town. Hank hadn't noticed or he would have said something.

At the sight of it there, any relief Colt felt now that the long nine-month wait was over and mother and daughter were doing well had gone up in smoke. He could speculate till doomsday about Geena's skittishness, but it wouldn't do any good until she told him what she'd been doing there. The hell of it was, he knew it was none of his business.

But he wanted it to be his business because he was growing more attracted to her all the time. The fact that she was planning to leave the ranch at the end of the summer was the very reason he should have no personal interest in her. Unfortunately, he'd already become emotionally involved with her.

She was the first woman to get to him like this since his divorce. He hadn't thought he could feel like this again. But alongside the attraction was the frustration that she hadn't opened up to him emotionally. Not being able to know her private thoughts and feelings was driving him crazy.

When he'd dropped off a taciturn Hank at the house, he'd gone straight to the barn for his horse. Since then, he'd been in the saddle close to eight hours repairing fence line. Hard work should have brought some semblance of calm to his mind, but nothing could have been further from the truth.

He walked into the mudroom to wash the dust off his face and hands. After drying himself, he stepped into the kitchen and was assaulted by the smell of roast lamb and homemade cinnamon rolls. The aroma knocked him back on his heels. It smelled like his mother's cooking before she'd come down with Alzheimer's. Since then Mary had taken over in the food department. Her meals had been good, but nothing like this.

His gaze moved to Geena, who was wearing a denim skirt and striped blouse her figure did wonders for. Her back was turned to him while she tossed a green salad. Everything was in order. The table set. *So what were you expecting, Brannigan?*

She turned to put the bowl on the table and saw him. "I didn't realize you were back. Congratulations on becoming an uncle!" Her cheery attitude got under his skin. Whatever she was hiding wasn't visible on the surface. "How does it feel?"

Geena had done nothing wrong. In fact, so far she'd done everything right. That was the problem.

"I'm still getting used to the idea." It was Hank who had the problem dealing with his emotions where Lindsey was concerned. "Where's everyone?"

Something flickered in the depths of her eyes, as if she didn't know what to make of his state of mind. "Hank said he was going out with a friend and left the house hours ago." That didn't surprise Colt. With the birth of the baby, his pain had intensified. "I'm sure Ina will be bringing your mother shortly. Would you like to eat now, or wait for them?"

He rubbed the back of his neck. "I'll see what's holding them up." But no sooner had he started for the hallway than they appeared. He smiled at Ina before grasping his mother's hand to lead her to the table.

For a moment Colt felt as though he was on the wrong side of a looking glass. When he peered in, he was in the same house he'd always lived in with the same delicious smells from the kitchen wafting through the air. But the mother he kissed showed no recognition of him or her surroundings, while the woman at the stove— He couldn't finish the thought.

Colt helped his mother to the table and Geena started to serve them.

Who was she?

He knew certain basic facts about her, but he didn't know *her* or what made her tick. She would have had women and men friends before her imprisonment. His stomach muscles tightened when he realized she might have had a lover at the time she was incarcerated. Hadn't she mentioned a boyfriend from before prison? In one morning she'd been torn away from everything she knew.

No matter what her circumstances were now, he couldn't figure out why she would need to talk to the police. If this had something to do with her imprisonment, she should be making inquiries with the authorities in Rapid City, not Sundance.

"This is another wonderful meal, Geena," Ina raved as she bit into another slice of roast lamb.

"Thank you."

"How did you learn to cook like this?"

"My grandmother." Colt was certain that was true. You'd never eat food like this in prison.

The new development with Geena had robbed him of his appetite. He ate a little, but was unable to do justice to the meal. After thanking her, he got up from the table. "If you'll excuse me, I need to make some phone calls for Travis I can't put off any longer. If someone asks, I'll be in the study."

It wasn't a lie. He'd told his brother he'd inform everyone about the baby, but he couldn't sit there in front of Geena and pretend everything was fine when it wasn't.

An hour later he went back to the kitchen for coffee. Before he reached it he heard voices and discovered Travis sitting at the table talking quietly with Geena while he finished his dinner. He must have been here for a while.

She'd done the dishes and stood at the counter drinking coffee with him as if they were old friends. Travis knew Colt had hired a new housekeeper. Judging by the way he was looking at her, his brother more than approved.

His glance lit on Colt. "I decided to take your advice and come home for a meal and some sleep before I go back to the hospital." His eyes returned to Geena. "This is a housekeeper worth keeping."

"Time will tell," she murmured, reminding Colt of their conversation about her position being temporary. She already had her life planned out once she left the ranch. But what was it? "Could I get you some coffee, Colt?"

"No thanks." Caffeine was the last thing he needed if he hoped to get any sleep tonight.

"I was just about to ask Travis where he fits in the family line," she volunteered.

His brother's tired face broke out in a smile before he got to his feet. "It's like this. Colt's our big brother. I was born three years later, and Hank came along eleven months after that."

"And now you have a darling baby daughter of your own," she commented. "I can't wait to get a peek at her."

"If all goes well, I'll be bringing them home before dinner tomorrow." He cleared his own dishes and put them on the counter. "After hospital food, that meal saved my life. I'm going to the cabin and will see both of you later." He left the house through the back door.

While Colt watched her, Geena promptly put the dishes in the dishwasher and turned it on before wiping off the table. She'd made the kitchen spotless.

"Geena?" He couldn't take any more of her seeming nonchalance. She looked up with those innocent eyes. "If you'd come to Travis's bedroom with me please." He needed to talk to her and didn't want Hank walking in on them unexpectedly.

CHAPTER SIX

GEENA followed Colt through the house to the upstairs, having felt tension from him the second he'd walked in the kitchen. He wasn't the same man who'd left for the hospital earlier that morning with Hank.

For that matter, Hank hadn't been in a mood to talk when he'd returned before going out again. Once he'd gone, there'd been no sign of Colt for the rest of the day and no appetite from him at dinner. She couldn't begin to understand the undercurrents in this house. The arrival of a new baby should have generated a certain amount of talk and excitement.

Colt took a left at the top of the stairs and led her to a spacious bedroom with an en suite bathroom at the end of the hall. An unmade baby crib with a mattress stood in the middle of the rustic room. Her gaze went to some sacks piled on the colorful quilt of the king-sized bed.

"They have a nursery set up at their house, but as long as Lindsey will be staying here for a few weeks, I called and had this delivered on Monday. Tell me…if you were a new mother just home from the hospital, I'd like you to look around with your woman's eye and see what else needs doing. Alice cleaned in here yesterday."

The man in charge of his ranching empire could do

anything, but a new baby in the house presented a challenge no one, including Geena, was prepared for. Her heart went out to Colt because in the Brannigan household, the buck stopped with him.

"Why don't we make up the crib first?" She walked over to the bed and emptied the sacks. The first thing that came out was a little pink tub. "This is perfect for bathing the baby."

Colt put it in the bathroom then helped her undo the packaging. Before long the crib looked like a dream with its pink and white padded bumper pad tied in place. "The pink hearts on that eyelet quilt are adorable. How did you know to pick anything so gorgeous?"

"I didn't," he said in a deep voice. "I ordered everything over the phone and said it was for a girl."

"Well the baby will love it. What's her name?" She'd been waiting to hear from someone.

"I don't know. They're still deciding."

That explained why Travis hadn't said anything. "Is Lindsey from a prominent family?"

"Yes."

"Here in Sundance?"

"No. Gillette."

"Since I heard from the men at the Cattlemen's Store that Brannigan is a revered name in Wyoming, she and Travis must be having a difficult time trying to decide which names from both family trees should be retained." For the first time tonight she glimpsed mirth in his hazel eyes. That was an improvement from his earlier mood and made her breathing come a little easier. "Let's put the crib against the wall out of the way."

Together they rolled it across the Oriental rug covering the hardwood flooring. Their arms and hips brushed against each other. Being in touching distance made it impossible to keep certain thoughts from filling her head. Like how would she feel if Colt were her husband and they were bringing home their baby.

Angry with herself for letting her mind wander, she hurried back to the bed. "She's a lucky little girl to have these cute stretchy suits and shirts. Where shall we put the clothes?"

"How about the dresser next to the crib? There's nothing in it."

"Perfect. We'll stack the diapers on top." In another few minutes everything was done. "When a girlfriend of mine had a baby a few years ago, the hospital sent her home with everything she'd need. If Lindsey's missing anything else, it won't be a crucial item. I'd say this room was ready. Let me just check the bathroom for towels. You can never have enough of them."

There were several on the racks. A quick check in the cupboards and she discovered half a dozen more. "Everything looks in great shape," she announced after walking back in the bedroom. "With a wastebasket in both rooms, Lindsey will want for nothing."

Colt had gathered up the mess into one bag to be thrown out. "Want to make a bet?"

A gentle laugh escaped her lips. He had a heightened sense of responsibility for everyone in his family and all living on the ranch. Maybe too much? Besides a marriage that had clearly ended, was this one of the reasons he didn't find the time to play or develop a relationship of his own?

"You work too hard, Colt Brannigan. Don't you ever take time off?"

He eyed her narrowly. "Probably not as much as I should," he admitted in a rare moment of truth.

"There must be times when you feel stifled by all there is to do around here."

Colt nodded. "Someone has to do it."

Like finding a new housekeeper for instance? The thought that his hiring her had been part of those things contributing to his feeling of suffocation haunted her.

With her work done here, she started to leave, but he called her back. "Was I mistaken, or were you parked in front of the police station this morning?"

Ah... He'd seen her. Naturally that raised questions and explained a lot. She turned around. "After going to the store and the post office, I stopped there on my way back to the ranch."

"Are you in some kind of trouble where *I* could help?" There it came again. That concern for her. If it was because he was personally interested in her, she'd have been thrilled. But she feared his natural drive to be in charge put her on his list of things to tend to.

Earlier she'd asked Colt to tell her if she did something wrong or stepped over the line. Now he deserved an answer. "No trouble at all, but since I'm freshly out of prison and work for you, I can understand your concern and realize you deserve an explanation."

He cast her a speculative glance. "As long as you're not in harm's way, you don't have to tell me anything." His sincerity made her pulse race harder.

True. She didn't have to, but this man had been so good to her, she'd never be able to repay him. The least she could do was put his mind at rest where her activities were concerned.

"I'm looking for someone who disappeared from

Rapid City without a trace. While I was in prison, I asked Kellie Tyre, a waitress friend of mine, if she could find out any information about someone I'm looking for. Kellie and I corresponded a few times, but she couldn't tell me anything.

"I never dreamed I'd get out of prison, but now that I'm free, I decided to stop at the police station to ask if they knew a good private investigator I could contact who would make inquiries for me. They told me I'd have better luck phoning a reputable attorney who could give me the name of one."

Shadows crept over his arresting facial features. "Is this person you're looking for a man?"

"No. As I told you earlier, the man I'd been dating at the time of my arrest, Kevin Starr, dropped me faster than he would have done a hot potato. Rupert's death was a hideous crime. Kevin has probably had nightmares over the fact that he ever dated me. The fact that he didn't once try to talk to me about it, or hear my side of the story isn't unusual. It would take a remarkable man who loved me deeply to at least make a few gestures." Someone like Colt...

"I'm sorry for that, Geena."

"Don't be. I expected nothing. Only a rare human being like you would ever have let me go into prison without at least wanting to know the facts from my lips. It's because of the way you're made." Geena loved him for that compassionate attribute.

"You don't know that."

"Oh but I do. You took me in, remember? As for the answer to your question, I'm looking for the woman who was living with my brother when he was killed. Her name is Janice Rigby. She'd moved into my grandmother's house with Todd while I was still in college at Laramie. When I came back to Rapid City for good, my brother told me I could stay with them while I was looking for a job.

"But Janice made me so uncomfortable, I went apart-ment-hunting and ended up renting from Rupert Brown. I didn't want to cause trouble for my brother. He loved Janice, so I never told him I thought she might be see-ing another man when Todd was out working the pipe-line. I have no proof, of course, but when I would go over there, she wouldn't let me inside and that made me wonder.

"Once in a while he and I met for lunch, but I didn't go near Janice because I knew she resented me. I'm sure he knew it too. Each time I was with my brother, I sensed he wasn't happy, but he didn't tell me why. We'd always been close. After I was put in prison, he tried to do everything to help me."

Colt came closer.

"When I heard he'd been killed, I thought, of course, that in her grief Janice would get in touch with me so we could mourn together. But she didn't. Not one word." Geena couldn't stop the trembling in her voice. "I need to see her and ask her about Todd. I don't know any details."

I don't even know if she had the baby.

"Kellie's last letter said Janice no longer lived in my grandmother's house. The landlord kicked her out along with some guy who'd moved in with her. I'd had my suspicions she'd been unfaithful to Todd. Apparently she left still owing the landlord rent and didn't leave a forwarding address."

His mouth became a taut line of anger. "I'm assuming she took off with all your possessions."

Geena bit her lip. "After I was locked up, Todd took all the things in my apartment back to the house. I'm sure Janice got away with the lot and probably sold everything to settle somewhere else. The furniture wasn't that important, but the mementos and pictures are priceless."

Instead of saying anything, she heard a groan from Colt before he pulled her into his arms. She knew it was a gesture of comfort. The milk of human kindness was instinctive in him. Though she should have eased away, he had no idea how much she needed this and slowly she felt her stiff body relax against his hard-muscled strength. While her body shook with silent tears, he rubbed his hands over her back.

She would never have expected this kind of intimacy from a man who held his emotions so close to his heart. Geena was totally unprepared for the feelings every stroke of his fingers evoked against her arms and neck.

When she realized he'd aroused her desire, she was appalled by her response and needed to stop this before she got in too deep and found herself clamoring for his mouth. How mortifying that would be when all he'd meant to do was lend her a shoulder to cry on. She'd known other men's arms around her in the past, but this was different. Entirely different.

Through sheer strength of will she took a step away from him. "I was afraid I might break down if I told you about Janice." Avoiding his eyes she said, "Thank you for being a wonderful listener. If I had to fall apart, I'm glad it was with you. The head of the Floral Valley Ranch has an unequaled reputation for handling the unexpected. I ought to know since I've already created several problems you didn't ask for." She moved to the door. "Goodnight."

Unasked for was right.
And you couldn't leave it alone, Brannigan.

Colt had thought her visit to the police station had been motivated by her involvement with a man prior to her imprisonment. Once again he'd gotten things wrong. Damn, damn and damn. But her explanation about this Kevin Starr explained why she kept so much to herself.

He'd thought he'd been wired last night....

Turning off the bedroom light, Colt headed down the hall to his room for a shower. A long cold one that would put out the fire her body had ignited in him like bolt lightning. When he'd doused every lick of flame, he would be ready to call Sheila.

Sheila was an attractive forest ranger recently stationed in Sundance. He'd met her a few weeks ago when a bunch of local ranchers had been called on by the forest service to help build a fire break. A fire in the western Black Hills needed to be contained. When it was out, Sheila had asked him to a party in town for this Saturday night given by the rangers. He'd told her he'd have to let her know later on because he wasn't certain when the baby would arrive and he might be needed.

But he had no excuse to turn her down now. The baby was here and the ranch had a new housekeeper who was more than holding her own. Colt ground his teeth. He would tell Sheila yes and have a good time, even if it killed him.

* * *

While the family had been assembled for breakfast Geena had been secretly relieved that Colt behaved as if nothing had happened last night. That was because the explosion of desire had all been on her part, not his. This morning he'd devoured his steak and eggs with relish before announcing that Lindsey's parents would be arriving any time now.

"Put them in the guest bedroom at the other end of the hall upstairs on the left. I'll try to get back to welcome them."

Geena nodded. She noticed Hank didn't say anything. Once Colt had left the table, he'd disappeared too.

After Ina and Laura had gone, Geena made up a batch of sugar cookie dough. As she was putting it in the freezer to get cold, someone else had joined her in the kitchen. This time Geena wasn't surprised. She turned to the woman in her mid thirties, "You must be Trish Hayward. I'm the new housekeeper, Geena Williams."

"Hi. Alice told me. She said you were very nice."

"Thank you, Trish." They shook hands. "I know you work around a schedule you've developed with Colt, but before you make beds and do the wash, will you come upstairs with me to the guest room? Lindsey had her baby."

"I heard it was a little girl."

"Yes. She and Travis will be staying here for a while and her parents will be arriving today. I want to make sure that the guest room and bathroom are ready for Mr. and Mrs. Cunningham."

"Sure."

They went upstairs and down the hall past Colt's and Hank's bedrooms. Both beds were unmade. Colt's looked thrashed, reminding her she was a restless sleeper too. Much as she would love to take a closer look at the pictures she could see on Colt's dresser from the doorway, she would never go in there unless she was given a reason.

His ex-wife must have been unforgettable for him not to have married again. Maybe this Sheila his brother had mentioned was someone important to him now. Geena didn't want to be jealous, but the mere thought of him holding another woman the way he'd held her last night sent a strange pain through her heart. This was what came from being locked away from men for such a long time.

Tomorrow was her day off. When she went to town to find an attorney, she'd drop by the store where she'd bought her Western gear and say hello to the guy who'd waited on her. If Steve was there and asked her out, she'd go and have a good time. She needed to do something to get Colt out of her system.

She and Trish went through the guest room to get it ready. The bathroom needed more towels and some things from the pantry such as hand soap and tissues. The closet had plenty of hangers and extra pillows. They'd need clean pillow cases. The bed needed fresh linens and the bedspread needed to be fluffed.

After leaving Trish to her duties, Geena went back downstairs in search of Ina and Laura. She found them taking a walk around the back of the house and joined them.

"Ina? I want to try an experiment with Laura. When you're through with your walk, would you bring her to the kitchen? I'm making some cookies to have on hand and thought Laura might enjoy helping me."

"That's an interesting idea. I'll bring her in a few minutes."

"Good."

When they appeared in the kitchen, Geena had made a place at the table to roll out a portion of the dough. She'd found a drawer full of cookie cutters and brought out the heart and the clover leaf along with a cookie sheet.

"Let's seat Laura right here. Colt told me she loved to cook. Maybe if she does a cutout and likes it, she'll do another one."

"It's certainly worth a try."

Geena got to work using the heart cutter first. It had a little knob that was easy to hold. She pressed it into the dough, then eased the cookie off the floured board with a knife and put it on the cookie sheet.

"Do you remember making these, Laura?" She put the cutter in the woman's hand and helped her press it down in the dough. After Geena lifted her own hand, Laura kept the cutter there and gave it another little thrust before lifting the cutter.

"That's perfect!" Geena cried. Before she could remove the cookie, Laura had found another spot and pressed all on her own.

"Well, what do you know," Ina marveled.

Laura was like a machine. Geena put the pan of cookies in the oven, then hurried to the freezer and brought out the other half of the dough to roll out. When she handed Laura the clover leaf to try, she hung on to the heart, her cutter of choice.

"It looks like you're having fun, Mom." Colt had come in the kitchen without them being aware of it and leaned between Geena and Laura to kiss her forehead. "Do you remember I like almond icing, too?"

Ina smiled. "Geena's idea is pure genius. I've never seen your mother enjoy anything this much."

Afraid the cookies were burning, Geena pushed herself away from Colt and rushed over to the oven to take them out. In truth, she'd felt the heat from his hard jaw searing hers. To her dismay he followed her and grabbed a paper towel so he could pick up a hot one.

"I haven't had a homemade sugar cookie in years." His gaze found hers and clung while he ate it in one go. "Mom used to make hearts and put our names on them."

"I tried to get her to use the clover leaf, but she didn't want it."

His eyes narrowed on her mouth. "That's because the leaves came unattached while we boys iced them. Wouldn't it be something if she still remembered?"

"If only more of her memories could come back," she whispered. If only Colt had met Geena under different circumstances and had asked her out because he couldn't help himself. Then she'd know that he had personal feelings for her. But she was the housekeeper, and she knew he was wonderful to everyone.

His eyes darkened with some unnamed emotion. "These cookies are delicious, by the way. Try one." He picked up another heart and put it to her lips, forcing her to take a bite. His fingers against her mouth sent curling heat to every atom of her body. While she munched he said, "Thank you for including her like this."

"It was an experiment. Since she liked it so much, she'd probably love some modelling clay. She could cut out cookies for hours."

"I'll pick some up and we'll try it with her." Maybe

it was a slip of the tongue, but his choice of words gave her heart a severe pounding. "I'm going to shower and change. By then the Cunninghams will have arrived. I'll settle them in their room and then drive them over to the hospital."

"Will they want a meal first?"

"Not until tonight."

She nodded. "I've planned dinner around food that should taste good to Lindsey."

"If it doesn't, it's Travis's problem." Meaning he'd have to deal with his wife in princess mode. Colt's tone had brooked no argument from Geena.

After he left the kitchen, she worked steadily to prepare everything and ice the cookies in Colt's favorite flavor. For dessert she made a lemon supreme pie. Anything chocolate might not be good if Lindsey was nursing.

Later, with no sign of anyone around, she went into the main dining room. The buffet yielded a drawer full of tablecloths. She found one in pale yellow and put it on the table. Since this was to be a welcome-home celebration for the baby, she went outside and picked some white daisies growing in the west garden.

She filled her arms with a large bunch and arranged them in two different vases from the china cabinet. One for the foyer table and one for the dining room. When she set it on the table with the china and crystal, it looked perfect. Now to get herself ready.

Once dressed in another skirt and top in dusky blue, she put her hair back in a French twist and fastened it with a clip. On her walk back through the foyer to the kitchen, she heard voices outside and opened the front door. Two cars had pulled up in the front drive.

Colt and Hank walked with Lindsey's smartly dressed parents, carrying flowers, suitcases and several bags of supplies sent home from the hospital. Travis helped his blond wife from the other car. Then he reached for the baby carrier.

When Lindsey's mother saw Geena inside the door, her gaze flew to Colt. "Who's this?"

"Our new housekeeper, Geena Williams."

She half laughed. "You're joking, of course."

Colt ignored her rudeness. "Geena? Please meet Martha and Jim Cunningham, Lindsey's parents."

"How do you do?" Geena smiled. "What a great day for all of you having a new baby in the family."

Mr. Cunningham eyed her with interest. "Indeed it is."

"Let me relieve you of some of this." She took the bags and flower arrangement he was holding. "I'll run these upstairs."

In Travis's room, she put the flowers on the bedside table and emptied the bags in the bathroom. They could arrange things the way they wanted. She took the empty bags with her and headed back downstairs, passing Colt on the stairs bringing up the suitcases. In a soft black shirt and tan trousers, he had an urban sophistication that showed her a whole new side of him.

His eyes penetrated hers. "The dining room looks amazing."

She couldn't stop her heart from thudding. "I hope it was all right."

"What do you think?" His question sounded fierce. "I told you to make this house your own. Everyone's speechless. The place hasn't looked like this since before Mother became ill and couldn't remember anything."

His compliment meant so much to Geena, she couldn't form words. Instead, she murmured her thanks and hurried on down. On her way to the kitchen, she saw that everyone had assembled in the living room. Travis had his arm around Lindsey, who was a beauty. She looked flushed and exhausted. Hank, not saying anything, sat across from Jim with his cast extended.

Martha held the baby, who, so far as Geena could tell, hadn't made a peep. She was all pink with fuzzy brown hair. So precious.

Ina sat on the loveseat with Laura. One grandmother stared into space while the other one took over. Geena felt a wrench in her heart before she moved to the other part of the house.

While she was making coffee, Colt entered the kitchen. "Lindsey's tired, so I think we'll eat now. She might not last through the whole meal."

"No problem."

After pouring ice water, she put all the food on the table where everyone could help themselves. Throughout the meal she poured coffee for those who wanted it.

At one point Lindsey's father glanced up at her while he was eating. "This is the best fried chicken dinner I've ever tasted."

"Amen," Colt agreed.

"Thank you."

Following their compliments Martha said, "Lindsey needs to go upstairs." With those words, the dinner ended and Geena could start clearing the table.

When all her duties were done, she put the dish towels and cloths in the washer. The tablecloth needed to go to the cleaners to be laundered and ironed. She'd take care of that tomorrow.

Geena came out of the laundry room at the same time Lindsey's mother entered the kitchen. "There you are." She sounded put out.

"You wanted to see me?"

"Yes. Tomorrow I'd like you to serve breakfast upstairs in my daughter's room at eight o'clock."

"For the four of you?"

"Yes. She'll want juice, bacon and toast. My husband likes his eggs over easy. I'll only eat a little cereal with milk and a grapefruit. Travis will want scrambled eggs."

"I'd love to accommodate you, Mrs. Cunningham, but Saturday and Sunday are my days off and I'll be away for most of it." The older woman's eyes rounded in surprise. "Fortunately I went to the store and there's plenty of food for you to help yourselves. When I'm back on Monday, I'll be happy to prepare your breakfasts the way you want."

She lifted her chin. "Mary was always on hand."

"I understand she was a paragon and is sorely missed. Before I go to bed, is there anything Lindsey needs for the baby or herself? A little snack maybe? I made some sugar cookies that might taste good. They're in that canister next to the toaster."

"I think not."

"Then if you'll excuse me, I'll say goodnight."

Geena had barely reached her room when she heard a knock on the door. She opened it to find Colt standing there. She guessed her heart would never get used to the sight of him.

"I saw Martha leave the kitchen like she was hurrying to a fire. Any problems?"

"None."

The hint of a smile hovered on his lips. "Tell me what happened."

"She didn't know I don't work on the weekend."

"That explains it." His eyes swept over her. "I know you've been waiting for tomorrow so you can visit your brother's grave."

Colt knew her well, but he still didn't know everything. If she told him, then he'd just take it on. She couldn't let him do that. He had more than enough on his plate.

"I was just about to phone you and talk to you about it. I don't feel good about taking the truck to Rapid City. Would it be all right if I drive it as far as Sundance? I could leave it in the parking opposite the bus station. After my return from Rapid City later in the day, I'll stop at the post office on my way back to the ranch."

He lounged against the doorjamb. "I have a better idea. Tomorrow I have some errands to run and want to get away early, so I'll drive you. We'll find a place to eat breakfast in Rapid City and spend as much time there as you want. On our way back through Sundance we'll grab lunch and I'll do my errands. How does that sound?"

Geena *knew* how it sounded. His asking to spend the day with her fed into her fantasy about them. If she agreed, it would be stepping over that line between boss and employee into more personal territory. Maybe that was what he wanted. Did he? Did she dare dream?

"It sounds like you're going out of your way for me again when I know you're needed in a dozen places at once here on the ranch. I'd feel better about it if there were some way to repay you."

"So far no one has any complaints about the new housekeeper. You've freed me to get on with ranch business, a luxury I haven't known for a long time and feared I might never have again. That's payment over and above what I expected."

Geena might have mapped out a long-term plan for herself for after she left his employ, but she hadn't counted on this attraction to Colt that was deepening by the minute. "Thank you," she whispered.

He stood straighter. "Meet me at my truck at seven-thirty in the morning and we'll escape before Martha comes looking for you."

Geena laughed quietly. "It seems rather cowardly just to slip away."

His eyes gleamed with devilment. "In some instances it's better to run for your life, don't you think?"

"If you say so," she teased. "You're the boss."

She'd said it without thinking because she was enjoying their conversation so much. But maybe it had been the wrong thing to say because the amusement unexpectedly left his eyes. In its place she felt tension.

"Is there anything you'd like to ask me before I go upstairs?" His polite question verified her suspicions.

"No." For some reason she'd offended him without meaning to. After he'd offered to drive her to Rapid City in the morning, she didn't want any misunderstanding between them.

But maybe she'd misread him.

Maybe she was being paranoid.

If so, it was because she was crazy in love with him. It shouldn't have happened. It was too soon for anything like this to happen, but there was no other explanation for why he lit her up like an explosion of fireworks just thinking about him.

"Then I'll say goodnight." He turned and strode down on the hall on those long, rock-hard legs. How would it be not to have to say goodnight to him? Oh, what she'd give.

CHAPTER SEVEN

FLOWERS decorated many of the graves at the Mountain View and Mount Calvary Cemetery. When they'd reached Rapid City, Colt had stopped at a florist so Geena could get the flowers she wanted. She ended up buying five baskets of spring flowers. Once they were off again, she directed him to the cemetery and found the family plot.

Her parents and her grandparents each had a joint headstone. Colt helped her carry the baskets to place against them. The last basket she put at the head of the unmarked grave. But when she leaned over, she sank to her knees as if her elegant jeans-clad legs would no longer support her.

"Todd."

That one name was said in such a heart-wrenching tone, Colt's throat almost closed off with emotion. Without conscious thought his hands closed over her blouse-covered shoulders from behind. He rubbed them gently while her body shook with quiet sobs he could feel resonate through him. All he could do was hold on to her while she unloaded her grief.

Colt had never met her family, but they had to have been remarkable people to have produced a daughter and granddaughter like Geena. He felt a terrible sorrow for her that she'd lost her only sibling. There was something about this woman that brought out his need to comfort her. *Face it, Colt. You want to love her.*

Though Colt had lost his father, his death had been easier to handle because he'd lived a full life. Todd Williams's life had been cut short, depriving Geena of her last relative, denying her that solace. She'd been in prison at the time, unable to do anything. Her pain had to have been unbearable.

Colt knew he couldn't relieve it, but there were other things he could do. When Geena finally stood up, he kept his arm around her shoulders. "Before we leave," he whispered against her cheek, "we'll talk to the sextant and arrange for a headstone to be made for your brother."

"I was just going to ask if we could do that. Thank you."

Still holding her, they walked slowly across the grass to his truck. He helped her inside and drove them to the office where she was able to order one. She put down a deposit using her credit card. They told her to expect a wait of a couple of weeks. When it was ready, they'd phone her.

After they were in the truck once more, he turned to her, struck once again by the stunning picture she made. A woman had to have been born with a soft curving jaw and classic features like Geena's to carry off the French braid she wore. "Have you tried to reach the man from the pipeline office?"

"Yes, but I learned Mr. Phelps has been out of town this whole week and won't be back until Monday." Her tears may have stopped, but she was still in an emotional state.

"I know you want to see him in person. When you've made an appointment, I'll bring you again. While we're at it, maybe you and I can track down this Janice together and you won't need a PI."

Her head jerked around in alarm. "No—I-I mean I couldn't ask you to do that," she stammered. "Please— you've already done too much for me."

Whoa. For Geena to have such a strong reaction meant she was still keeping something from him. "You didn't ask. I offered."

"But I'm only an employee."

He blinked. Last night she'd reminded him he was the boss. At the time it had gotten under his skin, which was absurd because it was only the truth. And yet he didn't feel like her employer. The lines separating them had been blurred from the beginning and they were getting more blurred all the time.

She wasn't like the help he employed on the ranch— not like a friend or relative. Geena had arrived on the ranch during the night and had gone to sleep beneath a pine tree. Titus had found her first. She was something else entirely different and growing on him in ways he couldn't explain. Colt only knew he was craving her company more and more.

He started the engine. "Before we leave Rapid City, would you like to run by your grandmother's house?"

She averted her eyes. "I don't think I could handle that today. I've done enough crying already, but thank you for being willing. You've been wonderful to bring me here. It's meant everything, but now I feel emotionally drained. If you don't mind, I'd like to get back to the ranch and I am sure you would too."

Colt had no doubts this had been a big morning for her, but he knew in his gut there was more to the story about Janice than she was willing to divulge. He wanted to help her, but he needed a way to gain her confidence.

"You wouldn't have any way of knowing I've taken the whole day off. Hank's in charge. Since you and I could both do with a break from our problems, how would you feel about going for a horseback ride with me when we return? I could give you a few pointers. We'd only stay out as long as you feel comfortable."

She glanced at him with a worried expression. "It's part of my job, isn't it?"

His hands gripped the steering wheel tighter. "No. Only if you want it to be."

He watched her bite her succulent-looking lower lip. "To be honest, I'm scared of them."

The bands around his lungs relaxed. "Why?"

"When I was little, my friend's father had horses. We'd go in the stable to look at them. One day I tried to feed this horse some hay, but I got too close and it kicked me in the ankle. I never went near horses again and still have a small scar."

Colt had to suppress the urge to pull her into his arms. He could hardly keep his hands off her.

"Then it's time you learned to feel comfortable around them, but only if you want to. We have a mare named Carrot Top who's gentle and patient. I could introduce you. The two of you could take a long look at each other and decide whether you want to take the relationship any further."

"Colt—" She half laughed.

He liked the smile on that gorgeous mouth of hers. It was her first one of the day. "By the time we've had lunch in Sundance and get back to the ranch, let me know your answer and it can be arranged."

"Up over this next rise you're going to see something spectacular."

While Carrot Top followed Colt's gelding, Digger, over terrain only a horse could traverse, Geena watched the play of muscles across Colt's back and shoulders. To her he represented masculine beauty in action.

After being in the saddle for a half hour, she wasn't nearly as nervous as she'd been. The grandeur of the scenery made this first effort of hers worth every second. And of course there was Colt, who'd been incredibly patient and gentle with her while he taught her the fundamentals of horsemanship. Earlier, when he'd unexpectedly pulled off her cowboy boot to see and touch her ankle scar with his fingers, the sensation had felt so erotic, she'd almost fallen out of the saddle.

She loved him with an ache that would never go away, but she was playing with fire and knew it. There was a price to pay for every minute she spent with him. Though she admitted they had chemistry between them, for her to think he had feelings for her beyond a moment's pleasure was ludicrous. Colt had been married once and since then had stayed single for a reason. That wasn't going to change. She was his housekeeper, for heaven's sake!

This day with him had gotten away from her, but if there weren't any more days off that included him, then she could prevent mistakes from happening.

"Oh—" she cried when her horse drew alongside

Colt's. She lowered her cowboy hat to the back of her neck and took in the scene before her. "It's absolutely glorious! Those wildflowers swaying in the high meadow—they're beautiful beyond description. No wonder Custer wrote about it. You have to be the luckiest man on earth to have all this in your backyard."

Beneath his hat he eyed her speculatively. "So you're not sorry I got you on a horse?"

"How could I be?" she answered in a breathless voice. "This makes you want to go up there and roll around in them." She regretted those words the second they escaped her lips. He probably thought she meant rolling around in them with him. He wouldn't have been wrong.

"You're a good sport, Geena Williams, but I think you've had enough for your first day. If I keep you out here any longer, you'll be cursing me tonight when you're too sore to walk."

Her lips curved. "Maybe, but I don't feel it yet."

"You will," he answered with a heartbreaking half smile of his own. "Next Saturday we'll ride clear to the top."

No. They wouldn't, because she wouldn't let there be a next time. Every outing with him would make it harder to be separated from him. If there came the day when he asked her to stay on the ranch because he wanted to marry her, well that would be different. But she couldn't imagine that happening and needed to keep her plans firmly in mind.

With a mental sigh, she urged her horse to turn around and follow Colt down the mountain. Neither of them were inclined to talk. Her thoughts were too full of him as she relived every moment of their day together.

By the time they reached the stable, she dreaded their separation. In fact she couldn't stand the thought of it, but to spend any more time with him was dangerous.

Another time today at the cemetery when she'd felt his hands kneading her shoulders, she'd come close to turning around and crushing herself against him. That would have been a serious error on her part considering he'd driven her to Rapid City out of his innate generosity and concern.

Before he could come around to help her, she got off her horse by herself. No more touching. Not any. "Shall I brush down Carrot Top?"

His gaze took in all of her, sending curling warmth through her from head to toe. "That's my job right now. What you need is a good soak in the tub."

At the mention of a soak, a picture of the two of them luxuriating together refused to leave her mind. "That sounds like a marvelous idea. Thank you for this, for everything. I'll see you later."

She practically ran down the hill to the ranch house. Once inside she hurried through to her bedroom, thankful she didn't see any of the family. After a quick shower, she changed into fresh jeans and a short-sleeved, filmy, melon-colored blouse. Donning her sandals, she was ready to leave again.

She hoped Colt was still at the barn and wouldn't see her drive away. Naturally when he walked down to the house, he'd notice the white truck was gone. But that was okay. She'd be back in Sundance, having put twelve miles between them.

When they'd been in the downtown section earlier today, she'd remembered seeing a beauty salon. After finding it now, she parked in front. The ad in the window explained they accepted walk-ins as well as appointments. She approached the girl at the counter who told her it would be a ten-minute wait.

No problem. Geena grabbed a magazine and thumbed through it, not really seeing anything. The day spent with Colt had been too memorable for too many reasons.

When one of the beauticians called to her, she put the magazine back and took a seat in the chair. "What can I do for you today?"

Geena looked at herself in the mirror. "I need a haircut." She hadn't worn it short since she was in middle school. "In my job I do a lot of cooking and always have to wear it in a braid like this or swept up. I used to have semi-curly hair. How about a tousled wavy bob to the neck with a part on the side so I don't have to think about it?"

"You have the perfect facial shape for it. Leave it to me."

A half hour later Geena left the shop feeling pounds lighter. It wasn't the weight of the hair gone, but the image. She liked her new look that had no association with the past and her prison photos. Communing with Todd this morning had helped free her of a lot of pain she'd been carrying around because she hadn't been able to say goodbye to him.

Again, it was Colt who'd been her fairy godfather. He'd done everything for her. She didn't know how she'd repay him, but one day she would figure out a way.

Until that time, she needed to concentrate on finding Janice without Colt's help. When she met with Mr. Phelps next Saturday, she'd ask him if he knew a good attorney who could steer her in the right direction. She'd ride her bike to Sundance. From there she'd take the bus to Rapid City. It had a bike rack so she'd be able to get around once she was there.

With her plan solidly in mind, she gathered the mail from the post office, then decided to drop by Bradford's Department Store where she'd purchased her Western clothes. If Steve was working, she'd say hello and see what happened.

But when she parked near the corner and walked to the store, she saw that it closed at five-thirty on Saturday. She checked her watch. It was quarter to six. As she walked away she heard a voice call to her. "Ms. Williams?"

Geena spun around. To her shock, there he was. "Hi! I'm surprised you would remember my name."

He grinned. "Are you kidding? I've been hoping you'd walk in one of these days. Are you with your boss?"

She chuckled. Steve could be forgiven for asking that question. "No. This is my day off. I had some shopping to do and thought I'd grab a quick dinner."

"What a nice coincidence. I was just leaving the store to do the same thing when I saw you through the doors. But I wasn't sure if it was really you. You've cut your hair. It gives you an entirely new look. I like it."

"Thanks. This style makes a nice change."

"How about walking around the corner with me to get a pizza? They're pretty good. There's a theater next door. We could catch a movie if you'd like."

"That sounds great."

Three hours later they left the theater. As he walked her to her truck he said, "I've been invited to a private party at the Lariat Club tonight. Some of the forest rangers are throwing it for the guys who helped them fight a fire a few weeks ago. Besides free appetizers, there's going to be a live band and line dancing. Come with me. Whenever you want to leave, I'll follow you back to the ranch to make certain you get home safely."

Steve was a very nice guy from Sheridan. She found out that since college he'd been working his way up in business management after being assigned to this store. Even if she was beginning to feel the aches and pains from her first horseback ride, why not spend a few more hours having fun with him? Anything to put thoughts of Colt out of her mind for tonight.

He asked her to follow his car to the other side of town. After she'd parked across the street from the bar and got out, she could hear the music coming from inside. Steve caught up to her. "Sounds like the party's in full swing."

The place appeared to be packed. He ushered her through the crowd to the dance floor. "Let's do this before the band takes a break."

Geena hadn't been line dancing since her last date with Kevin Starr from FossilMania. Steve knew all the moves. His energy infected her. For a little while she simply went with the country-and-western sound, hardly able to believe she was a free agent instead of wasting away at the prison in Pierre.

When the music stopped, Steve's smiled faded and he got the oddest look on his face. "Maybe I'm seeing things, but I think the ranger who invited me to the party is coming this way with *your* boss."

Colt was here?

Geena's heart thudded so fast, it almost suffocated her.

"Hey, Steve—I'm glad you could make it. Who's your friend?"

Of necessity Geena had to turn around. Her gaze collided with Colt's. The gold flecks among the green of his eyes flashed molten as he took in her new haircut. She could feel the tension emanating from him to her bones. Unless his feelings for her ran deeper than she'd supposed, it made no sense. Oh Colt…if that was true…

"This is Geena Williams. She's the new housekeeper on the Floral Valley Ranch. Geena? Meet Sheila Wilson, one of the forest rangers assigned to Sundance."

The blonde woman nudged Colt in the ribs. "You didn't tell me that job had been filled. You're a dark one, you know that?" She turned back to Geena with an alluring smile. The ranger was good at covering up her feelings, but Geena had witnessed her shock knowing that she lived under the same roof with the man Sheila had invited to the party.

"It's nice to meet you, Sheila."

"I'm glad you could come. The more the merrier." Her blue-eyed gaze swerved to Steve. "How did you two meet?"

Steve moved closer to Geena, as if he were establishing his territory, but there was no contest for going up against Colt. In the coffee-colored shirt and jeans he was wearing, no man would ever compare. "I helped her buy a new outfit."

Colt studied Geena for a moment longer, but she couldn't read the expression in his eyes. "I take it you bought something else this afternoon." His voice sounded an octave lower than usual.

She shook her head. "No. I told Steve that the next time I came to town, I'd stop by and say hello. We've just come from a movie." She'd decided to tell the whole truth because Colt deserved nothing less. And if that bothered him, then why didn't Colt ask her out?

"If you'll excuse us, we're going to grab some hors d'oeuvres." Steve put a hand at the back of her waist and led her to a table near the front. Even in the crowded room Geena felt those piercing hazel eyes staring at her back. Colt would be able to tell she was having some difficulty walking after their horseback ride.

"Let's get out of here, shall we?" Steve whispered at last. She nodded. Seeing Colt here tonight had shattered her plan to try to forget him for one night. The whole evening had been ruined. She knew it. Steve knew it.

They walked across the street to her truck. The cool air met her hot cheeks. When they reached the driver's side, he put a hand against the door to prevent her from getting in. "Do you want to tell me what's going on with your boss? If looks could kill—"

"He didn't look at you like that!" she cried.

"I'm talking about the way the big rancher was looking at *you*, as if you were his property." Steve really thought that? "It was the same way he acted the other day. Tell me the truth, because I don't like to play games. Are you two involved?"

She lowered her head. "Not in the way you're thinking. I'm just his employee, but it's complicated."

If she explained about her false imprisonment, she had no doubt Steve would understand why Colt came off so protective around her. Todd would have been the same way. But Steve wasn't the man she loved, so there was no point in leading him on, let alone telling him about the horror of the past year.

"You're telling me," he muttered. "Do me a favor. If it ever gets uncomplicated, you know I'm interested."

"I'm sorry, Steve. I never meant for this to happen tonight. I'd hoped to spend an evening with you and was shocked when I saw Colt with Sheila."

"The other day she told me she's had a crush on him since she first met him. I think seeing you pretty well explained why their relationship has never gotten off the ground."

"I've only been at the ranch a week."

"Sheila fights fires and would tell you it only takes a single spark to ignite one."

That's what it had felt like that night in his kitchen. Colt had taken pity on her and had offered his hospitality. When she'd looked at him, something had leaped between them. Call it a spark. Whatever it was, she'd been on fire since then.

She sucked in her breath. "Thank you for the dinner and the movie. No matter what you think, I had a great time and enjoyed your company very much. Otherwise I wouldn't have come by in the first place."

"I believe you." He nodded and opened the door so she could get in. "I'll follow you home."

"No. It's only nine-thirty. Not that late. I only have twelve miles to go. Steve—I saw quite a few girls inside without partners. Go back in the bar and have a good time."

"Don't worry about me. See you around, Geena."

She'd hurt him, darn it.

Jabbing her key into the ignition, she started the engine and took off for the ranch. Colt had turned her whole world around today. Maybe she should give her notice, then work for the next three weeks to earn the money he'd already put in her account. After that she'd get on her bike and ride out of his life. Thanks to him she had some new clothes and a little money to find work somewhere else. In time there'd be more money. She just had to wait.

Once she'd turned off the highway onto the dirt road, she saw headlights behind her. It appeared Steve had decided to follow her home anyway. She wished he hadn't, but he was one of those nice guys who didn't deserve a situation like this.

She pulled in next to Hank's truck and got out of the cab. To her dismay she walked right into a wall of steel. "*Colt*—I thought it was Steve behind me."

His mouth had flattened into a thin white line. "Sorry to disappoint you."

Her brows furrowed. "I'm not disappointed. In fact I asked him not to follow me, but I *am* shocked to see you here when I know you were Sheila's date."

"Let's just say everyone's night was pretty well ruined."

"Because of me?" Her voice shook. "Is *that* what you drove all this way to tell me?"

"No," he said in a wintry tone.

"Then what's wrong?"

"I wish to heaven I knew."

"I think you were precipitous in hiring me. While you find the right housekeeper, I'll finish out my first month before I leave. How does that sound?"

A bleakness stole over his chiseled features. "I thought you wanted the job."

"I do, but you were the one who stated the arrangement was temporary in case one of the parties wasn't happy about it. As I see it, you already find me the wrong fit."

"Did I say that?" he challenged in a grim voice.

"In a way. You're angry as blazes right now."

His hands shot out to cup her hot face. "Maybe it's because after the day we spent together, it shocked me to see you enjoying yourself with someone else."

She'd asked him for honesty. He deserved it back. "You think I felt any different when I saw you there with *her*? On the day you hired me, Hank said you were busy on the phone with a woman named Sheila. That's why he took me to your mother's room to meet her instead of waiting for you. I wondered if she was someone important to you."

His fingers tightened in her hair. "I've never been out with her. The only reason I told her I would meet her at the party was to be polite. But as you can see, I couldn't even spend a whole evening with her once I saw you." His eyes lit everywhere. "You've cut your hair."

"I've wanted to change it since I got out of prison."

"Either way, you're a beautiful woman, Geena, and I have to have this before I take another breath."

His mouth closed over hers before she could stop him. Her hunger for him was so great she didn't want to stop him. He pressed her body against the truck with his and kissed her in so many different ways she groaned in ecstasy. Geena forgot where they were. She wrapped her arms around his neck in order to get closer. For a while she went where he led, giving him kiss for kiss, wanting to merge with him.

Her body literally trembled with desire. He had to have felt it and eventually relinquished her mouth. While she tried to catch her breath, he covered her throat with kisses before burying his face in her hair. "Tell me what really happened after you were arrested. When Kevin didn't make contact, are you afraid he ran off with your brother's lover?"

What? She couldn't believe what he'd just asked her.

"No, Cole—" He had the wrong idea completely. "I never felt that way about Kevin. When I was away at college, I fell in love with a man and thought we would get married. We had several classes together and it was a wonderful time in my life. But I found out through a friend that he'd been lying to me all along and was only separated from his wife, not divorced."

Cole held her tighter.

"He told me it was only a matter of time and begged me not to leave him, but I was too devastated by his lie to consider going back to him. I eventually got over it and dated other guys, including Kevin, after returning to Rapid City, but there was no one special. It's hard to get your trust back after you've been betrayed."

His hands slid up her arms and he shook her gently, forcing her to look up at him. "You don't feel you can trust me?"

"You know I do!"

"Then explain to me why you won't let me help you find the woman who stole your possessions."

"Because it's not your problem and I don't want to be any more of a liability than I already am. You've felt sorry for me and have done more for me than anyone else would have done. You told me you've been overwhelmed at times by all the responsibility."

"What are you talking about?"

"I'm not your typical woman who answered an ad for a housekeeper. You think I don't know your family has questions about me? You may not be harboring a fugitive, but if they knew who I was, I'd be a person of interest to them in the wrong way."

His jaw hardened. "I was right," he said in a savage whisper. "You need counseling to help you. Have you called that psychiatrist yet?"

"No, and I'm not going to. I'll find my own closer to home when I'm ready." She'd look for a P.I. online, too, and go from there.

"You're not telling me something," he ground out. "It means you're afraid."

"I could accuse you of the same thing," she threw back at him.

His dark brows furrowed into a bar above his eyes. "Explain that to me."

"Except for one reference about you giving up steer-wrestling after you got married, that's all I know about your personal life. I never asked questions about your former wife because I didn't feel it was my right."

After a long silence he muttered, "Touché," and let go of her arms.

She fought for composure because it appeared he still wasn't ready to confide in her about the most crucial time in his life. "Why don't we both agree this isn't the right fit for either of us? I'll work hard for the next three weeks before I leave. Hopefully you won't have any complaints."

In the semidark she thought his features had taken on a gaunt cast. She imagined her own complexion was probably the color of paste.

"Before I forget, here's your mail." She opened her bag and handed the bundle to him. "Goodnight, Colt."

Geena couldn't get away from him fast enough.

When she entered the kitchen, Hank was there drinking coffee. She flew past him, returning his "Hi" over her shoulder, and kept on going to her bedroom.

Shaken by the passion that had flared between them, Colt stood there for a few minutes in order to recover. When he could finally move, his legs felt as heavy as that vital organ pumping blood through him—blood that needed to cool so he could think rationally.

He'd blown it, but there was no way in hell he would let her leave the ranch in another three weeks. They both had trust issues, but after a year behind bars, hers had to be worse. Unfortunately he'd come off acting like her bodyguard, pushing everyone else away while he kept her close. In the process he feared he'd alienated her.

Determined to set things right between them, he stormed into the house. Ignoring Hank, who stared at him in astonishment, he strode down the hall to her bedroom and knocked on the door.

"Geena? It's Colt. I need to talk to you for a minute."

After a pause he heard, "If you don't mind, I'm exhausted. Could we do it in the morning at breakfast?"

Colt exhaled a heavy breath. "Tomorrow's your day off."

"I'm not going anywhere, so I'm planning to make the breakfast Martha asked me to make for everyone this morning."

His hand absently made furrows through his hair. "You don't have to do that."

"I know. I want to. Maybe Lindsey will let me hold her baby. I've been dying to do that." He heard a wobble in her voice that got to him. Everything about her got to him.

"If you'd told me, I could have arranged it."

"I know. You can arrange anything."

There he went again, trying to micromanage her life. The last thing he wanted was her resentment. *So what do you want, Brannigan?*

The answer terrified him for fear she didn't want the same thing.

His eyes closed tightly. "Get some sleep, Geena."

He turned on his heel and walked away, making a tour of the house to lock doors and turn off lights. Only by sheer strength of will did he eventually head up the stairs instead of finding his way back to Geena's room.

Hank was there, sitting on one side of Colt's bed with his legs extended. The two looked at each other. "What's going on with you and Geena?" his brother asked, point-blank.

Colt shut the door before backing against it. "I'll answer that question when you tell me what's been happening to you? I thought whatever went on between you and Lindsey was over before she started dating Travis."

Lines marred Hank's face. "It was over—for *her*."

That answered one of Colt's questions anyway. "What are you going to do about it?"

"Listen, Colt. I know you've needed me for the last six weeks. But after I get my cast off on Monday, would you care if I flew straight to Casper? Robert called here earlier to ask about the baby. We got talking about other things. Before I knew it he invited me to come for a visit if I wanted to. How about if I stay there until Travis and Lindsey have moved back to their house? Some time away might help me to get my head on straight."

Colt walked over to the desk and tossed the bundle

of mail on it. Then turned to his brother. "I think it's a great idea. He'll like having you around, too."

A look of relief crossed over his face. "Thanks, bro." Hank got to his feet and hobbled over to give him a hug. Colt hugged him back hard, wanting Hank to get past this. If he met the right girl in Casper... No doubt Robert was thinking the same thing.

"Our cousin is the best friend a man could have next to his own brothers." Colt's thoughts flew to Geena, who needed her brother. Colt wanted to be there for her, but *not* as a brother. Kissing her tonight had turned the fire into a near conflagration.

When Hank reached the door, he turned to him. "Maybe after I get back, you should do the same thing and spend some time with Robert. Geena has you more fired up than the bull that went after me."

His brother had *that* right!

CHAPTER EIGHT

GEENA glanced at the wall phone in the kitchen. She picked up the receiver and pressed the digit for the upstairs guest bedroom. Martha answered on the third ring. "Lindsey?" she asked in an anxious voice.

"No, Mrs. Cunningham. It's Geena. I have breakfast ready for all of you. Would you like me to serve it in your room or your daughter's?"

"Oh—I thought you'd be away like you were yesterday, but no matter. Bring it to our room. We'll eat around the table. Be sure there's sugar for my cereal."

For a moment Geena felt like Cinderella being given her instructions for the day. "I'll be there shortly."

After clicking off, she found one of the largest trays and stacked it while Ina and Laura ate their breakfast. On her way up the stairs she prayed she could manage the feat as well as Cinderella had done in the feature film.

Jim stood at their open door in pajamas and a robe with a big smile on his face. "Aren't you a sight for sore eyes! I hardly recognize you with that new hairdo. It's very very becoming."

"Thank you, Mr. Cunningham."

"I'll let Lindsey and Travis know breakfast has arrived. I've been salivating for more of your food since dinner the other evening."

"That's so nice of you to say." She swept past him and put the tray on the coffee table. Martha was also dressed in a robe, brushing her hair. Her eyes swept over Geena but she made no comment.

"I hope you brought enough food for me." *Colt's voice.* She swung around. Unlike the others, he'd already gotten dressed. In jeans and a white polo, he was so handsome in his rugged way, she could hardly take her eyes off him, but she *had* to.

"If not, there's more downstairs."

He grabbed a piece of bacon off the plate. "Um. Crispy, just the way I like it. Why don't I pop next door and see what I can do to get everyone assembled while this food is still hot?"

It was a good thing she hadn't seen him as she was coming up the stairs or her body would have gone weak, causing her to drop the tray. While she was still trying to recover, Colt came back in the room holding Travis's daughter. Her heart leaped at the sight of him with a baby in his arms.

He walked over to her. "Geena? Meet Abigail Cunningham Brannigan, my niece and newest member of both families. Abigail was Lindsey's grandmother's name," Colt informed her.

"How wonderful to have that connection."

Geena's gaze fastened hungrily on the baby wearing a tiny pink stretchy suit. She was wrapped in a receiving blanket. "Oh—she's absolutely adorable." When he handed the sweet-smelling baby over, Geena heard a muffled sound of protest from Martha, but it was too late. Colt had made certain Geena got the opportunity to hold the baby. She loved him for it.

The baby's eyes were open. Her mouth had formed into a perfect O. "You dear little thing. Welcome to the world, Abby." Unable to resist, she kissed her cheek, then held her against her neck and shoulder. The warmth of her little body tugged on all Geena's motherly instincts. She wanted one like this of her own.

With Colt for the daddy.

She couldn't stop thinking like that and started walking around the room, wondering what had happened to Janice. Had she delivered a healthy baby? Was it Todd's? Had he made Geena an aunt? Or was it another man's child? With this baby in her arms, Geena knew she had to find out the answers and she needed to do it soon.

Fighting the tears that had already moistened her eyelashes, she turned to Colt and handed the baby back to him. "Thank you for letting me hold her." Her voice was so thick with emotion she needed to get out of there.

"If there's anything else you want, phone me in the kitchen," she announced to the room, then hurried out the door. Lindsey and Travis were just leaving the other room in their robes. Geena kept going. They'd already met her. She was the hired help after all.

When she reached the kitchen, she discovered Hank at the table. She'd made plenty of food and he'd helped himself. His eyes brightened when he saw her. "I think I'm going to have to marry you to keep all this fabulous food in the family."

Her laugh was bittersweet. If Colt had said that to her...

"You seem happier today."

"I am. My cast comes off tomorrow and then I'm taking a short vacation."

"Where are you going?"

"Casper."

At the mention of it, guilt swamped her because she'd turned down Colt's suggestion to speak to the therapist there. To make things worse, he unexpectedly strode into the kitchen. "Did you save any food for me?"

"There's plenty," Geena assured him. "Sit down and I'll serve you."

She made him a big plate and poured both of them coffee. While he and Hank talked, she cleaned up the kitchen. In a minute Hank brought his dishes over to the sink. "If anyone wants to know, I'm leaving for the day. Danny's picking me up."

During her horseback ride with Colt, she'd learned Danny worked as Hank's hazer when they did the rodeo circuit. "Have a good time. Just think—tomorrow you'll be given your get-out-of-jail-free card."

"After what you survived for a year, I can't complain about six weeks' deprivation."

She stared at Hank in shock while Colt looked at both of them stone-faced. "You know?"

He nodded. "I sensed something was fishy the night Mandy and I walked into the kitchen. The next day when you told me you'd been hired, I wondered if it had anything to do with that call from the warden. So I called Warden James back." The expression in his eyes softened. "She told me what'd happened to you."

So Colt had kept his word. His good deeds just kept mounting up to the most marvelous man in the entire world. "And you didn't mind too much?"

"Sometimes innocent people get blamed for doing

bad things. What was there to mind? I told you the other day you're the best thing to happen to this ranch in years! The warden told me she was relieved to hear Colt had hired you. She's been worried about you and hopes you'll get all the help you need after what you've been through."

He flashed her a sly grin. "It was one decision I'm thankful my big brother made. By the way, I love your hair. See ya later." Hank gave her a kiss on the cheek before he left the kitchen.

"Geena," Colt murmured, "will you please sit down for a minute? I'd like to talk to you."

"All right." Last night he'd been upset. This morning his mood was completely different. Benign, for want of a better word.

"Can we start over again?"

Her head went back. "What do you mean?"

"Exactly what I said. The warden had the right instincts from the beginning. You do need all the help you can get in order to pick up the strings of your life again. I'm afraid I've tried to solve them for you all at once."

Colt was breaking her heart. This was probably the closest thing to an apology she would ever hear from his lips, but he didn't owe her any apology. Quite the opposite. She owed him everything!

Her fear now was that he was apologizing for those minutes in his arms last night. She'd wanted it to go on and on. The thought of it never happening again was too terrible to contemplate.

"You can't help it," she teased with a quick smile. "That's why you're the head of the ranch. Everyone loves you and looks to you. This place would fall apart without you. I admire you more than you know." *I love you more than you know.*

Lines bracketed his mouth. She'd forgotten he didn't like compliments. "Nevertheless, to make up for my heavy-handed behavior, I'd like to do something you'd enjoy. I feel like playing." He winked at her, reminding her of that other conversation they'd had. "Have you ever been to Devil's Tower National Monument?"

"No, but I've heard about it all my life." The idea of doing anything with him was so exciting she couldn't sit still and got up from the table to clear his dishes.

"It's a sacred place to the Lakotas where they perform the Sun Dance. June in particular is a time when most tourists are encouraged to honor their tribal traditions and don't try to climb it. But we're free to visit. Since it's a beautiful Sunday and we both have the day off, how about we put our bikes in the back of my truck and drive there?"

"You have a bike?" She sounded excited by the possibility.

He nodded. "I think mine still works. We'll pedal around and see the sights, then move on to other places and eat as we go." She heard his chair scrape as he got up from the table. "If that doesn't appeal, then tell me now and I'll get busy working on the books for the accountant who'll be here next week."

A whole day with Colt? It's what she'd been wanting all along. *Quick, Geena, before he withdraws his invitation and leaves.* After she'd turned on the dishwasher, she flashed him a glance. "I'd love it."

Eleven hours later, after doing the whole tourist-attraction loop through the Black Hills, Colt drove them into

Hulett, a town nine miles from Sundance. He parked near the White Pine Inn before ushering Geena inside for the best steak dinner this side of the Continental Divide, according to the sign. They had a great live band and dancing. He'd been waiting all day for this. If he had to wait five more minutes to get her into his arms, he was going to explode.

Once they'd been shown to a table and had given their orders, Colt asked her if she wanted to dance. The old Colt would have swept her into his arms without getting her permission, but he was on his best behavior and it was paying dividends. He felt they'd passed the point of no return today, they were no longer just boss and employee, but something more.

"I'd like that. It all depends on if my legs can handle it. We must have pedaled miles and you don't even show it. That has to come from working in the outdoors from sunup to sundown."

He hadn't been doing a lot of that since Geena had come into his life. Mac told him the ranch hands were beginning to wonder where he'd disappeared to. "Which exercise was more painful for you? Riding Carrot Top or your bike?"

"My bike, I think." She chuckled. "But if you're willing to take a chance on me, I won't say no."

The news was getting better and better. He moved around the table and walked her to the dance floor. No line-dancing here. With the soft rock playing in the background, Colt could get close to her so he felt every line and curve of her body. That's what he needed. To feel her molded to him and to breathe in her fragrance. She intoxicated him.

After several dances, he looked into her face, trapping her eyes so she wouldn't look away, but he caught her tearing up. "Are you too sore for this and haven't told me?"

"No," she answered quickly. "A week ago I was lying on my prison cot trying to figure out how to make my life count for something. I just didn't know how. If someone had told me that before long the Good Samaritan would rescue me and show me the time of my life, I would have known I'd gone insane."

He cocked his dark head. "Good Samaritan?"

"Yes. That's you."

Intrigued by the analogy he said, "In that case, what prevents you from allowing me to do something else good for you? I'm trying to improve my image as a whole-loaf guy. You could help me with that by letting me into your confidence a little more. You're fighting tears. I noticed you doing the same thing earlier while you were holding the baby. What did Abby's presence trigger in you?"

Her body quivered. That reaction told him he was getting closer to the secret she was keeping from him.

"When I saw you holding her, Colt, it reminded me that Todd's life had been cut short and he was denied the privilege of becoming a family man."

Colt felt she was telling him the truth, just not all of it. "Do you know, when I picked her up out of her crib, the first thing I wanted to do was show her to Mom and Dad? My divorce took its toll on the family. I think they despaired over any of their sons producing grandchildren."

"Oh Colt—" One lone tear trickled down her flushed cheek. "I'm being so selfish thinking only of myself and my sadness. I'm sorry." Their mouths were mere inches apart. She gave him a brief kiss on the lips before easing herself out of his arms. "Our dinner's waiting for us."

The touch of her mouth stayed with him after they settled down to enjoy their meal. Once the waitress brought dessert, Geena shot him a question he hadn't anticipated. Not tonight anyway. "Did you ever bring your wife here?"

He put down his fork. "No."

"Tell me about her. I've seen the family pictures on the walls, but you're always with family or friends, not one special woman. I'm filled with curiosity. How long were you married? What was her name? Where did you meet her?"

Colt lounged back in the chair. "Why do you want to know?"

"Why do you think?" she fired right back, then grinned. It was the grin that caused him to cave. "I'm a typical woman who wants to know everything. It's the way *we're* made."

He couldn't refuse her. "Maybe on the drive home."

"Good. I'm going to hold you to that. It's a woman's prerogative and this woman wants to know what makes the great Colt Brannigan tick."

He danced with her a few more times, but the direction of their conversation had changed the tenor of the evening. Though he could tell by the way she nestled against him that she loved moving to the music with him, she wanted something else from him. When the band took a break, he asked her if she'd like to stay.

Geena shook her head. "I'm ready to go."

Halfway back to Sundance, they reached the turnoff for the ranch. He drove them past the house to another road that took them up through a ravine lush with summer grass and foliage. No one would bother them here.

He parked at the side of the dirt road and shut off the engine. "I brought you to this spot because it's darker here. If you look up at the sky, you'll see the constellations better."

"My first night out of prison beneath your ponderosa, the Big Dipper seemed so close I could reach up and touch it. It was a heavenly night."

Colt stirred restlessly while he studied her profile. "Until Titus and I came along and ruined it for you."

She turned to him with the hint of a smile. "Once my heart rate settled back to normal, I didn't mind. Especially after you invited me inside the house when you could have ordered me off your property. The way the ranchers at the feed store talked, I assumed you were a man of probably fifty or so.

"Instead I was confronted by this much younger, attractive, modern-day knight in boots and jeans who'd rescued me from a dragon. You took my breath away. I kept wondering why you couldn't have come sooner and stormed my prison in Pierre."

Geena.

"I think I've been very patient waiting a whole week to hear about the woman who captured your heart. Naturally she would have been beautiful. Probably small and delicate, the kind that brings out a man's protective instincts. Blond maybe, with warm chocolate-brown eyes and a complexion like porcelain. How am I doing?"

"Make it strawberry blond and you've described Cheryl."

"Ah. You have to watch out for those strawberry varieties. Nature endowed them with that particular advantage over the rest of the female population. How young was she?"

"Twenty. I was twenty-one."

"And you were both smitten at first sight."

He examined her features in the moonlight. "That's the word for it," he said, concentrating on the woman next to him. "Nothing cerebral. Just pure hormones raging out of control."

"I'm sure there was more to it than that."

"Not really. It was the proverbial case of opposites attracting."

She eyed him speculatively. "Then she wasn't a farming girl?"

"No. The daughter of a surgeon from San Francisco."

"I see. How did you meet?"

"It was June. She was on vacation with several of her college friends. They'd driven to Reno for some fun and decided to take in a rodeo. Their first. I won my event that night and they were in the crowd to congratulate me. I stayed over to spend the next day with her."

"How long before you got married?"

"Six weeks."

"That fast—"

"Yes, ma'am. She followed me to some other rodeos on the circuit. By the time we reached Elko, I couldn't concentrate on anything. We decided to get married in San Francisco. My family flew out for the wedding. We took a two-week honeymoon in Hawaii on my latest winnings, then I brought her home to the ranch. We lived in the house Travis and Lindsey are in now."

"I can guess the rest," Geena murmured. "She hated the isolation and missed her friends."

Colt's gut twisted because he realized Geena had to

be feeling the same way since her imprisonment. She'd been uprooted from everything. He cringed to remember she'd had her life literally torn away from her.

"Cheryl wanted us to move to California so I could find a good job."

Geena gave a caustic laugh. "She certainly didn't know the real Colt Brannigan, did she? You could no more turn your back on your family and your Wyoming heritage than fly."

Neither could Geena forget her heritage when she was a South Dakota girl through and through.

He'd offered to drive her by her grandmother's home, but she'd refused because it would be too painful. More than ever he understood why she'd insisted on the housekeeper job being temporary. In time she hoped to recover certain mementos from the past and make her permanent home in Rapid City.

If anyone deserved to get her life back it was Geena. Haunted by what she'd lived through, Colt was going to help her whether she wanted it or not.

He started the truck and found a spot where he could turn around. She was silent all the way back to the house. Before they got out of the cab he turned to her.

"Tomorrow morning I'll be driving Hank to the clinic early so the doctor can remove his cast. We won't be eating breakfast. After that I'll fly him to Casper. He's going to spend some time with our cousin Robert. I probably won't be back until Wednesday. If an emergency should arise, Mac's in charge, but you can always phone me. If all else fails, there's Travis."

"Thanks for telling me." She opened the passenger door. "I'm glad for Hank. He needs to get away."

Colt grimaced. "In case you didn't guess that too, he thinks he's still in love with Lindsey."

After a pause, "They have a history?"

"Two dates only before she refused him a third one. Later on in the year she met Travis at a party by accident and they fell in love."

Geena nodded. "That explains his moroseness. The poor guy needs to settle down with a woman who has loved him for years. Like Mandy perhaps?"

His eyes squinted at her. "What are you saying?"

"Well, you have to admit she's been a good sport to chauffeur him around with his foul disposition since the cast was put on. It isn't friendship she wants. Hopefully one day soon he'll realize a relationship with Lindsey was never meant to be and he'll take off the blinders. Mandy hasn't been biding her time for nothing over the years you know."

Colt burst into laughter. "How do you know so much about everyone in such a short time?"

"That's easy. I've been in prison observing women for over a year. Somehow Mandy has learned to appreciate all Hank's wonderful qualities lying beneath that sinfully good-looking exterior of his. In the looks department all three of you Brannigan men were given more than your fair share," she added.

So saying, she jumped to the ground. "Have a good flight both ways and come home safely," she whispered. "The Floral Valley Ranch couldn't go on without you."

The last thing he saw were her imploring inky blue eyes shimmering in the moonlight. They put a stranglehold on him before she closed the door and vanished.

CHAPTER NINE

WEDNESDAY morning Colt left his uncle's ranch and flew from Casper to Rapid City to see Lieutenant Crowther, the detective who'd broken the case for Geena.

Colt sat across from him at his desk. "As I told you on the phone, Geena's brother, Todd Williams, passed away while she was in prison. I'm trying to help her find the woman who was living with her brother at the time of Geena's arrest. She'd like to recover some of her possessions. Do you know anything about her?"

The detective nodded. "Geena insisted she'd been framed and gave the public defender the names of everyone she could think of. Janice Rigby was among the list of suspects I compiled while I was trying to reconstruct the facts of the murder. I'll let you look at the rap sheet on her. She has an alias." He printed out a form on his computer and handed it to Colt to read.

Five years ago Janice had been arrested and served a one-year jail sentence for possession of marijuana in Leadville under the name Angie Rigby. After that there was a list of petty thefts throughout towns in the Black Hills area. Her last arrest had put her in jail for fifteen days. It had happened while Geena herself was in prison.

Colt raised his head. Somehow this woman had hooked up with Todd and used him like a bank because he'd been willing. Geena had loved her brother. He dreaded the thought of telling her what he'd found.

"When Geena first met Janice, she thought the other woman was involved with a man besides her brother, but a rap sheet like this means she had an addiction to drugs that started years earlier and this is only the tip of the iceberg. She probably sold every possession of Geena's and Todd's to support her habit."

The lieutenant's brows lifted. "I'm afraid so. I doubt she's in Rapid City now, but I'll tell you what I'll do. I'll run a search through the national database and see if there's new activity on her reported in other counties or states. If I find out anything, I'll let you know in case Geena is still interested in finding her. Give me your phone number."

They traded information.

"One more thing," the other man said. "There's a piece of news not included on the rap sheet. With this last arrest, they did a physical on her. She was six months pregnant."

Pregnant?

Colt shot out of the chair. Geena had to have known, but she'd never said anything to him about it. "I had no idea."

"Given the woman's record, maybe the baby wasn't her brother's and that's why Geena never told you."

"True." But maybe the baby *was* Todd's. If there'd been a live birth, Geena might have a niece or nephew out there somewhere. Getting back her mementos was one thing, but the possibility that the baby was Todd's would explain her desperation to catch up with Janice. Suddenly it was all clear to him.

"Thank you, Lieutenant. You've helped me more than you know."

Colt called a taxi to take him to the airport for the short flight back to Sundance. After being away from the ranch for any reason, home always called to him. But as he set down the Cessna and started up the truck, he forgot there was a speed limit. It felt like months, not days, since he'd last been with Geena.

To prove to himself she didn't matter to him, he'd purposely refrained from phoning her and had stayed in touch with Travis and Ina instead. But his experiment had backfired on him and he could hardly breathe as he parked the truck and hurried inside the ranch house to find her.

The house looked immaculate and was quiet as a tomb. He strode down the hall to his mother's room and heard voices coming from the veranda. When he stepped outside he found Travis and Lindsey eating lunch with Ina and their mother. Colt greeted everyone and kissed his mom who was still enjoying her food. "Where are your parents, Lindsey?"

"They drove to Gillette for a big party, but they'll be back this weekend."

Jim had probably gotten antsy sitting around.

"You're looking good. Where's the baby?"

"After Geena made lunch for us, she volunteered to tend her until her next feeding in order to give us a breather."

Travis eyed him. "Geena's amazing! As you can see, there's still plenty of food here. Sit down and tell us how Robert's doing."

"Actually I've had lunch and there are some things I need to do, so I'll fill you in at dinner."

He left the veranda and hurried through the house to the staircase. Taking the steps two at a time, he raced down the hall to Travis's old room expecting to find Geena, but she wasn't there. Colt checked the other upstairs rooms to no avail.

That meant she was in her room.

With his heart pounding like a sledgehammer, he went back down and took a few deep breaths outside her door. Afraid to knock for fear he'd wake the baby if she was asleep, he carefully turned the handle and looked inside.

Geena lay in the center of the bed facing the door. The carrycot sat on the floor. She'd put the baby next to her and was studying her the way a mother would do. Her face was awash in tears. He might have been mystified if he hadn't talked to the lieutenant. Moved by her pain and the tenderness she showed the baby, he entered the room and closed the door, then tiptoed over to the bed.

Abby was sound asleep. When Geena saw him, he heard her quick intake of breath.

"Lindsey told me you were watching her," he whispered, "so I thought I'd let you know I'm back. I hope it's all right I came in."

"Of course. Everyone must be glad you're home safely."

And you, Geena?

He leaned over. "She's beautiful, just like her mother."

Geena's wet midnight-blue eyes looked haunted. "I don't think I've ever seen a more perfect baby."

There was someone else Colt had never seen anyone

more perfect than. She was within touching distance. Unable to help himself, he picked up the baby and settled her in the carrycot, then he stretched out on the bed next to Geena. When she would have gotten up, he put out his arm and rolled her back into him.

He buried his face in her hair. "I've just come from police headquarters in Rapid City and know about Janice's pregnancy. Why didn't you tell me?"

She eased away enough so she could look at him. "I thought you were in Casper."

"I left there this morning and took a detour before coming home. I know you wanted to hunt for Janice on your own, but it's too late for that. After seeing her rap sheet, we're in this together from now on. There are some things you need to know about her."

"Besides her being involved with another man?"

He sucked in his breath. There was only one way to say it. "She spent a year in prison five years ago for possession of marijuana. Since then she's been in and out of jail several times for petty theft. If you think I'm going to let you go without me to look for her, then you don't know me at all."

"Yes, I do," she said on a moan, clutching him to her. "Only too well. That's why I hoped you'd never find out. When you hired me, you didn't know you'd be taking on so much responsibility. It isn't fair to you."

"Stop talking about fair, Geena. I want to help you, and the detective's going to do what he can to locate her. He'll be phoning me by the end of the week."

She shook her head. "I wish this hadn't happened. Now you feel a new obligation to help me. It's all you do and I don't want to be any more of a burden than I already am."

"If you're a burden, then it's news to me. Right now I'm going to kiss you, Geena. If you don't want me to, that's tough. No quarter asked or given you said. Remember? Your mouth is all I've been able to think about since you kissed me on the dance floor in Hulett."

His hand spanned her tender throat, positioning her face so he could plunder her mouth. He'd been starving for her. It was ecstasy to feel her crushed in his arms like this. He tangled her long gorgeous legs with his and kissed her over and over again. They rolled from side to side on the bed, finding new ways to bring pleasure to each other.

Ages later he pulled her on top of him. "I want to make love to you, Geena, and I know you want it, too."

"I don't deny it," she cried softly, kissing him back with a passion he'd never known in his life. This woman didn't have a selfish bone in her body. When she gave, she did it so completely he felt transformed.

Colt traced the voluptuous line of her lips with his finger. "Maybe some Friday night we could ride up into the mountains and camp out where we can be alone and look at the stars. We wouldn't come back till Monday morning."

She kissed every centimeter of his face. "Who would look after your mother and Ina?"

"Travis."

"How easily you say that when we know I was hired for that very job and more."

He bit her earlobe gently. "Your job is what I decide it is," he growled. "If that shocks you, I can't help it. You bring out the primitive in me. It's your fault. Ben White Eagle calls it 'woman magic,' sent down from the gods when a man is searching for his vision. According to him such magic can make him whole and guide his path."

She kissed his hair where she'd been running her hands through it. "Do the Lakota women have visions of 'man magic'?"

Her question delighted him. "I don't know. Why don't you ask Alice?" he asked against her lips before feasting from her mouth once more.

"I think I will. She's going to help me clean the pantry shelves on Friday."

"After that you'll need a nap. I can help you out with that, too." Once again he was lost in euphoria and forgot everything else. "You smell and taste divine, Geena. Did you know that? I think I'm never going to let you leave this bed."

"Not even to return Abby to her mommy? In case you didn't notice, she woke up a minute ago and wants to be fed."

If Colt had heard the baby, he'd been too entranced by Geena to think about anything else. But Abby's cries were growing louder, bringing an end to rapture he couldn't get enough of.

The tap on the door brought Geena to her feet. Colt was slower to respond and didn't get off the bed fast enough before Travis popped his head inside the room. Their eyes met in an unspoken message while Geena ran around the end of the bed. "Abby's been asleep until just now. I'll change her first."

"There's no need," Travis said. "I'll do it. We really appreciated the help. Lindsey was able to take a little nap." He lifted the carrycot from the floor.

A blush had swept up Geena's face. Travis wasn't blind and would see she'd been kissed senseless. Her blouse was no longer tucked into the slim waist of her jeans. It was all Colt's doing, but he didn't care. Slowly he got to his feet. "Looks like it's your shift, bro."

"Yup," Travis answered with a grin. "Thanks. You make a great babysitter, *bro*." He left, pulling the door shut.

Geena glanced at her watch. "I-I can't believe it's almost five," she stammered. "The baby slept for such a long time."

"She's a Brannigan and knows when to keep quiet for her uncle."

"Colt—" She laughed, but he knew she was embarrassed.

"Whatever you're thinking, just remember Travis knows I came looking for you and will realize I'm the one who took advantage. Your reputation is still impeccable."

The animation left her eyes. "As long as he knows we don't make a habit of this."

"Now, there's a thought." Colt didn't like being brought back to reality so fast. "What are we having for dinner?"

"Barbecued ribs and scalloped potatoes."

"In that case, I'll be back in two hours." He forced himself to walk to the door without grabbing her in the process. "After we eat, I'd like to spend time with Mom. I picked up some clay in Casper and thought we'd try out your idea."

"I'd love to see what she does with it. Yesterday I put her to work shucking corn."

There was no one like Geena. "Did she do it?"

"Oh yes. Perfectly. I gave her eight ears. I think she

got upset when there weren't any more to do. Tomorrow I'm going to see how she does shelling peas."

Colt knew he had to get out of her room before he threw Geena over his shoulder and took off to the mountains with her.

Geena went into the bathroom to freshen up. Abby had made the perfect chaperone. Her cry had brought Geena to her senses barely in time before Travis was at the door. Her tiny presence had prevented Geena from making the biggest mistake of her life. If she slept with Colt, she would be the one who ended up with a heartache that would never go away.

Colt had married the woman who'd stolen his heart. When it didn't work out, he'd retired it. There was no plan for another marriage in his future, but since he had a housekeeper who was madly in love with him, they could indulge in lovemaking whenever the opportunity presented itself.

Nope. That wasn't the way it was going to happen while she worked for him. She was the temporary help and didn't want him in the role of rescuer-lover. Her white woman's vision was more spectacular than that.

If by some miracle she caught up with Janice and found out she'd had the baby, Geena would go from there. No matter the outcome, she couldn't stay at Colt's and live off his generosity. Hopefully by the time her first month was up, she would have received the money from the state and would be able to leave his employ having fulfilled her contract. For now she'd make certain he didn't regret hiring her.

After she'd served dinner, Colt said, "Ina? I'll take

care of Mom and put her to bed. Feel free to do whatever you want."

The other woman looked thrilled. "Thanks, Colt. I'll be on the phone with my sister in Gillette if you need me."

Once she left the kitchen, he brought the modeling clay to the table for his mother and rolled out the red color with a glass. Once Geena had done the dishes, he asked her to sit down and play with them. She got three cookie cutters out of the drawer and put them in front of Laura. When his mom picked up her favorite and kept making hearts, he lifted eyes full of gratitude to Geena. She knew what he was trying to tell her.

Still trembling from the look he'd given her, Geena rolled out the blue dough. Without missing a heartbeat, Laura started in on it. Colt quickly rolled out the yellow. "I don't think Mom has had this much fun since the onset of her disease."

"She does it all with such perfection. What a wonderful woman she must have been to raise such devoted sons."

"Mom was the best." His husky tone spoke volumes.

They worked on until ten o'clock. He finally put his hands over his mother's. "Come on, Mom. I'm sure you're tired. Let's go to bed."

"I'll clean this up," Geena volunteered. "Goodnight, Laura."

He flashed her a penetrating glance. "Thanks for making this a memorable evening for her and me. The ribs were fabulous, by the way." With a kiss to Geena's unsuspecting lips, he took hold of his mother's hand. She got up from the table and he walked her out of the kitchen, taking Geena's heart with him.

Over the next two days she saw little of Colt and felt the loss. To handle it, she kept busy with her normal routine and spelled Ina off by taking Laura for walks around the ranch house. The new assistant, named Joyce, came on Thursday. Geena liked her upbeat disposition. She would work two days a week, plus one weekend a month. This would be a huge help to Ina.

On Friday morning Alice arrived and they went into the pantry to get to work. Halfway through their project Alice smiled at Geena. "You work hard like Laura used to."

"I do?"

"Yes. Colt's the same way. He's a great spirit."

"I agree," Geena said in a quiet voice. "I'm very lucky to work for such a generous man."

"That's because he has the soul of a Lakota inside him. He walks in harmony with Mother Earth where all things are related. Colt respects nature and is in balance with it."

"Those are beautiful words, Alice." *For a beautiful man.*

After they'd finished their work, Geena thanked Alice and then left for town. On the drive she thought about Colt's ex-wife. How little she'd understood him. You couldn't uproot Colt. It would be unthinkable. This was a man who matched his mountains—solid and forever. Her whole body ached with love for him. That was why she needed to leave his employ soon.

Once she'd done the grocery shopping, she stopped to pick up the mail. There was an envelope for her in the pile! Her hands shook as she opened the letter sent to her from the state of South Dakota. Inside was a check for $75,000.

The letter said, "This is reimbursement for your thirteen months of false imprisonment. It could never replace what you've lost, but it's my hope it will bring you some solace. Good luck to you in the future, Ms. Williams." It was signed by the governor.

She hugged it to her chest. This money would help her begin a new life independent of Colt, who'd saved her life up to now. After depositing it in the bank, she drove back to the ranch full of plans. Tomorrow she'd ride her bike to Sundance and catch the bus for Rapid City. There were people she needed to see.

For one thing she could pay Todd's back rent to the landlord. For another, she wanted to talk to her waitress friend Kellie. Maybe she knew someone who'd known Janice and could help track her down. Colt had told her the detective was looking into it, but Geena could do it too now that she had the means.

She returned in time to fix lunch for Laura and Ina. Dinner came and went, but there was no sign of Colt. They were moving the herd to the higher pasture. He probably wouldn't be home until time for bed.

Geena had just settled down for the night under her covers when the phone rang. "Colt?" she said after seeing the caller ID. "If you're hungry, I put your dinner on a plate in the fridge wrapped in foil."

"That's music to this starving man's ears. I'm on my way back to the house, but wanted to catch you before you went to sleep. Tomorrow morning I'm driving us to Rapid City. We have two appointments. Mr. Phelps is going to meet us at ten in his office. Afterwards Detective Crowther is expecting us to come to police headquarters."

Her heart raced. "Then he must have news about Janice—"

"I'm sure of it."

"But he didn't say if it was good or bad?"

"No. Since we're going that far, why don't you pack an overnight bag? We'll stay at a hotel so that we can have dinner and take in a film tomorrow night."

She moaned at the dangerous thought of being alone with him like that. "Colt—I—"

"I'll book separate bedrooms if that's what's bothering you."

"It's not!" she cried, but that wasn't entirely true. "I happen to know you have other things to do with your time and—"

"Goodnight, Geena. I'll see you out at my truck at eight o'clock. Don't take off early on your bike and force me to track you down like I had to do last time." He clicked off.

She bit her lip. He read her mind with frightening ease.

After breakfast at the hotel restaurant in Rapid City where Colt had checked them in to adjoining suites, they drove to the pipeline company. Mr. Phelps, who looked to be in his fifties, greeted them at the door of his office. Geena caught his hand in both of hers.

"Thank you for meeting with us when I know you don't have office hours today."

"I'm happy to do it, Ms. Williams. Won't you and Mr. Brannigan be seated?"

"Thank you."

The other man eyed her kindly from behind his desk. "When I heard you'd been exonerated, nothing could have made me happier. A great wrong was committed at a time when you were grieving for your brother."

Her throat almost closed with tears. "You have no idea how long I've been wanting to visit you. There aren't enough thanks in this world for what you did for him. To know you gave him a decent burial next to my family—" Moisture glazed her eyes. "It was the only thing that helped me through that dark time. You're a wonderful person, Mr. Phelps, and I'm going to pay you back every penny."

He shook his graying head. "I wouldn't accept it. Todd's accident happened on the job he was doing for us. Of course we paid for his burial. It was the least we could do. He was one of the hardest workers in our company and a very fine man, totally dependable and reliable."

"That was Todd."

"Everyone liked him and has missed him."

"I've missed him too." She felt Colt's hand grasp hers.

"In his file you were listed as the next of kin."

"One who was in prison," she whispered, "but you found me and made everything right. I'm very grateful."

"I wish I could have done more. Mr. Brannigan told me all your possessions are gone, even mementos and pictures. In light of that, I had this made up for you." He handed her a file folder from the top of his desk. "It's the picture he gave us when he made out his application for work. It's been blown up in color."

Geena opened the folder. A small cry escaped to see her smiling brother the way he'd looked a few years ago. "Oh—this is a wonderful picture of him!"

"He was a very handsome man. Obviously good looks abound in the Williams family."

She smiled, but could hardly see Mr. Phelps through the tears. "I'll treasure this forever. Bless you, Mr. Phelps." She cleared her throat. "We won't take up any more of your time."

As she got to her feet, he came around and gave her a fatherly hug. "I hope you can put this behind you now and get on with your life."

Geena looked at Colt. "With Mr. Brannigan's help, that's exactly what I'm doing. I'm finding out there are many Good Samaritans in this world."

Colt gave her arm a squeeze before escorting her out to the truck. The second they were inside, he leaned across the seat and put his arms around her. For a few minutes she had a good cry. "Sorry. I've gotten your shirt all wet."

"Do you really think I care?" He kissed her cheek, then with seeming reluctance he let her go before starting the engine. "Would you like to head back to the hotel before we drive to the police station?"

"No, but thank you for offering. This picture of Todd has made everything so real again. I have to know about Janice one way or the other."

CHAPTER TEN

No ONE was more aware of Geena's need to find out about the baby than Colt. He drove over the speed limit to reach police headquarters. The tall, rangy detective was waiting for them. Geena's eyes fastened on him. "You're the one responsible for my freedom, Lieutenant Crowther. Do you mind if I give you a hug?"

Colt saw the male admiration in the man's eyes before he said, "Not at all." He hugged Geena back. "I only wish the DNA evidence had turned up sooner to spare you more grief."

"Looking at it from my perspective now, thirteen months compared to sixty years doesn't sound like much."

"Only enough to change your life," he added on a perceptive note.

Geena eased away and sat down in front of his desk. "Colt says you have news for me about Janice."

His expression didn't reveal anything. "That's right."

"I need to find her and the baby if it's possible."

He sat forward in his chair. "It's possible, but you won't have to go looking."

"Why not?"

"After running her name through the database, I

discovered she'd been taken into custody some time ago and is now imprisoned at the women's facility in Pierre."

"What?" Geena's gaze swerved to Colt in shock.

"In January of this year eight members of a gang were arrested in Sturges, South Dakota, in a drug bust. She and her boyfriend were among that gang. The charges against her included theft of cash, possession of drugs, operating in a cocaine facility, distributing cocaine inside a school zone to name a few. Because of her prior felonies, she was sentenced to twenty years."

"Oh, how awful—" she blurted in pain. "What about the baby?"

"She delivered a girl born at Mercy Hospital here in Rapid City on November the sixth."

"A little girl?"

"Yes. She was born prematurely and kept in the hospital due to complications of drug addiction."

"I was afraid of that."

"Two months later Janice was arrested."

Geena groaned. "Where's the baby now?"

"At a group home here in Rapid City."

"So close? But what about visitation? It's a long way to Pierre from here. Who takes the baby to her?"

"There's been no visitation because she signed away her parental rights. When she declared that the father was deceased, she named you as the one remaining relative who might be interested in the baby. But she said that you were in prison and it seemed unlikely you would make a custody claim, since you'd been sentenced to sixty years."

The detective sent Colt a look. "In anticipation of our meeting, I ordered DNA testing done on her. As for your brother, the hospital took a sample of his DNA when he was flown to the hospital after his accident. They ran the tests for me and both came out a match, Geena. She's *your* niece. I've already alerted Mrs. Wharton at social services who's involved in this case. She now has all the particulars."

Geena's ecstatic squeal filled the whole room. She leaped out of the chair straight into Colt's arms. He caught her to him while she sobbed for the second time that day. He knew what this news meant to her.

When she'd recovered, she turned to the detective. "Can I see her?"

"Of course. I told the person in charge to expect you. The baby is in a facility run by the St. Francis convent as part of their outreach program. I've written down the address for you." He handed it to her.

"I know where this is." She lifted star-filled eyes to Colt. "We're only five miles from there."

"Then let's go."

The detective saw them to the door. "Good luck to you, Geena."

Tears streamed down her face. "Thank you for being you, for being there at the right time and the right place for me. I'll never forget you for as long as I live."

Colt watched the detective swallow hard. "Days like this make it worth it."

He'd taken the words right out of Colt's mouth. To see Geena this happy on the inside changed her entire countenance. If Colt himself could ever make her this happy...

They hurried out to the truck and she told him where to drive. It wasn't long before they reached the grounds of the convent and pulled around to the main doors marked for visitors. Once they went inside, there were arrows pointing the way to the group-home area. Colt grasped her hand while they walked down a hallway to the glassed-in reception room.

A sister looked up from the desk. "May I help you?"

"My name is Geena Williams, and this is my friend, Mr. Colt Brannigan." At least Geena hadn't called him her employer, but the word *friend* didn't cover what he felt for her. "I'm here to see a little girl Lieutenant Crowther told me you have. I just found out she's my niece."

The older woman smiled. "Oh yes. He phoned to tell me you were coming and he has alerted the social worker working on this case. Please sit down."

"I understand the baby was sick after she was born."

"I'm afraid so. Because she came two months prematurely, her lungs were underdeveloped and the drugs in her system almost took her life. It was a fight for quite a while, but she finally started to do a little better. She's still not thriving the way the doctor would like to see. For a seven-month-old, she seems closer to five."

Geena looked stricken by the news. "Are you saying her mental capacity has been affected, too?"

"No, no. But she's taking longer to catch up physically. The doctor said it was normal in these situations. We try to pay as much attention to all the children as we can, but we have a full nursery. Most people wanting to adopt are searching for a healthy newborn."

Colt knew Geena couldn't take any more waiting. "Could we see the baby, Sister?"

"Of course. I'll bring her to you."

Geena's complexion had taken on a pallor he didn't like. "You heard the sister. The baby is fine. She just needs some good old TLC. Sometimes a new colt struggles at first, so you baby it and talk to it, feed it more often and pretty soon it's prancing around like all the others."

A glimmer of a smile appeared. "You're right. I'm so thankful you're with me, Colt." She reached for his hand and clung. His pulse raced because it was one of the few times she'd taken the initiative with him. He'd been waiting for her to act on her own with him. "I couldn't have done this alone."

"I'm glad you didn't have to."

Before long the sister appeared with what did look like a five-month-old infant dressed in clean unisex overalls and a shirt too big for her thin frame. He watched Geena's eyes clap on her niece.

"I don't believe it," she cried softly when the sister lowered her into Geena's arms. "Oh, you darling little thing. You've got your daddy's brown hair and blue eyes, but the rest of you is Janice."

Not all. There was enough of Geena's beautiful mouth and chin thrown in the mix to tug at Colt's heart. The baby's lower lip quivered and she started to cry.

"Have I frightened you? I'm so sorry. I'm your Aunt Geena and I love you to death."

Colt knew that.

She put the baby against her shoulder and rocked her until she calmed down a little. "Sister? What's her name?"

"We have no idea, but we've called her Lori."

"That was my mother's name! How did she come by it?"

"I'm told that when the baby was taken to the hospital, this was wrapped in the blanket." She handed her a tiny gold charm with the name Lori inscribed.

"This is my charm, the one my grandmother gave to me to remember my mother!" She showed it to Colt. "Todd must have found it among my things."

Colt nodded. "Janice may have sold off everything else, but she had enough of a conscience to save this when she gave up her baby and mentioned you."

Tearing up like crazy, Geena got to her feet and started walking around the room while she cuddled her niece. "Lori is the perfect name for you, my little darling. Lori Louise Williams." She turned a beaming face to Colt. "Louise was my grandmother's name. The one who raised me."

By now Colt had joined them. He kissed Lori's nose. "She's a real beauty, just like her aunt." He pressed a kiss to the side of Geena's neck so she wouldn't forget all about him. Her answering quiver meant she was still aware of him.

"Sister? Would it be possible to keep her for the weekend?" The pleading in Geena's voice was too much for Colt. "We'll be staying at a hotel tonight. I want to get to know my niece."

"You don't live here?"

"No," Colt asserted. "Geena makes her permanent home with my family as housekeeper on the Floral Valley Ranch outside Sundance. It's just over the South Dakota/Wyoming border less than two hours from here.

"Since Geena is Lori's only living relative and plans to adopt her, she'd like to take her home immediately so the bonding can begin. We have our own doctors in Sundance and the ranch is already equipped with a nursery. Is there any reason why we can't take her with us right now?"

A big smile lit up the sister's face. "None at all. When the detective called, I told him I hoped this would be the result. If you'll drive over to social services now, you can make formal arrangements for the adoption with Mrs. Wharton. Then you can come back and pick up the baby."

"We'll do it!" He turned to Geena. She looked as if she'd gone into shock. The good kind. "After we meet with Mrs. Wharton, we'll check out of the hotel and run by a store to buy a car seat and carrycot for Lori. The rest we'll figure out when we stop for dinner in Sundance with our new little bundle." He kissed her mouth.

"Colt—" He could see the gratitude brimming over in her eyes. But he also heard the worry in her voice. This was one time he didn't want to listen to all the reasons she couldn't let him do this for her.

In three weeks Lori was blossoming. Now that Travis and Lindsey had moved back to their house, Lori had inherited the crib. She loved the pink hearts and reached for them and the figures hanging from the Mother Goose mobile Colt had bought.

Geena was delighted to see her little body had started to fill out. She wiggled and smiled all the time, especially when Colt was around. He was supposed to be the hard-working head of the ranch, but Geena swore he spent more time with her and Lori in her bedroom than anywhere else.

She would never forget what he'd told her about nurturing a sickly colt. Hands down he made the perfect father. Whether it was feeding Lori her bottle, holding her over his shoulder when she threw up, diapering her, walking her at night when she cried, he was right there to help. Clearly there were two women in Geena's bedroom who worshipped the ground he walked on.

When the next Wednesday rolled around, he took over feeding Lori while Geena prepared breakfast for the family. After everyone had eaten and disappeared, he got up and put the baby over his shoulder to get out any burps.

"Geena? I'm flying to Casper on business in a few minutes. I won't be back before Friday. I'll be bringing Hank home with me."

"I'm sure you can't wait for his help again."

"That goes without saying." He looked tired. That was because he did everyone else's work plus his own. It was too much. "Mandy's going to be happy, too. You know you can call me any time, and Travis is here for you day or night."

She'd been loading the dishwasher. It was a good thing her back was turned to him because she was afraid to look at him right then. He'd done more for her than any human being could be expected to do, but there was just one thing wrong with this picture.

He's not your husband, Geena, and he never will be.

"I know," she said without turning around. "Be sure to fly safely."

"I plan to take extra care. Lori's going to miss me, aren't you, sweetheart?"

"Of course she will. You've spoiled her."

"She shouldn't be so beautiful. That's because she takes after you. It's a good thing she's too young for me to worry about boys flocking around her," he said before leaving the kitchen.

Geena couldn't take his banter any longer, not when he wasn't the marrying kind. The time had come to carry out her plan. She'd been thinking about it since the day they'd brought Lori home, but it had never seemed the right time to leave his employ until now. The only way she could consider doing it was because Lori had given her the one reason to go on living without Colt.

She'd taken the housekeeping job not knowing what the future would hold. But the reality of the baby had changed everything. Geena had already signed the necessary papers and was waiting for the adoption to go through. Even if Colt were to tell her he'd like her to stay on indefinitely as the housekeeper, he hadn't expected her to bring a baby under his roof. No, no.

Once he'd left the house, she picked up the carrycot and took Lori to her bedroom. She had just enough time to pack up and write him a letter before Alice arrived to clean. But Geena had another job for Alice to do as soon as she got there.

"Where's the fire, bro?"

Colt made a grunting sound. "I've been gone two days." Once they left the airfield, he drove the truck faster.

"If there were something wrong, Mac would have phoned," Hank reasoned. "I thought you said everything was fine when you talked to Geena last night."

"That's what she said, but I'm not so sure."

"You think Mom's sick? Or Lori, and she's not telling you?"

"I don't know, but I'm sure as hell going to find out." Geena had said all the right things during his two conversations with her. And yet something had been missing and he didn't like the vibes he was getting.

When they reached the ranch house, Colt levered himself from the cab and rushed inside the house. He headed straight for his mother's room with Hank trailing. They found her and Ina out on the veranda. All seemed well.

After he kissed her and had a small chat with Ina, Colt walked through the house to find Geena. The first red flag went up when he saw Alice going up the stairs. This wasn't her day to work.

"Hi, Alice."

She turned around. "Hey, Colt."

"What are you doing here today?"

"Helping out."

Her non-answer made him totally suspicious and he headed straight for Geena's bedroom. When he walked in, he realized it had been vacated. Everything looked exactly as it had before Geena had arrived on the scene. No remnants of the baby or Geena. Nothing...

Sick to the core of his being, his eyes darted to the dresser where he saw an envelope propped next to some keys. Hardly able to breathe, he took the steps necessary to reach for it, then sank down on the side of the bed. When he opened the envelope and withdrew the letter, a wad of money fell out. The sight of it produced pain more excruciating than the horns of any rogue steer that had ever gored him.

Dear Colt—

How do I begin to thank you for all you've done for me? I had a talk with Alice a few weeks ago. She said you were a great man born with the soul of a Lakota. Your life is in harmony with the earth and all things living, giving you balance.

I agree with her. Everyone comes to you because you're wise and generous, and so good it makes me cry. It's been my privilege to know you. As we said in the beginning, the contract was temporary. But things got out of balance when I found Lori and she was able to come home with me. You told the sister I had a permanent home with you, but it wasn't true. That wasn't part of the contract, so I've moved on.

Alice said she would fill in as housekeeper until you can find a permanent one. I hope you won't be upset with me for that. She loves you and she's wonderful. Best of all, she knows how to take care of your home and your family better than anyone else.

The money is payment for the two months' salary you've given me along with all the extras. I was no housekeeper and didn't earn a dime of it. You took me in out of the kindness of your heart. You let me play house and cook. You clothed and fed me in my hour of need. All of it brought me joy beyond description.

I wish you great joy in the future. Above all people, you deserve it.

God bless you, dearest Colt.

Geena.

Colt crushed the letter in his hand before he flew from the room out of breath. *"Alice?"*

He checked his movements when he saw her standing at the other end of the hall. "Yes, Colt?"

"Where is she?"

"The last time I saw her was in Sundance at the used-car dealership," she answered, calm as the summer day outside.

Geena had sworn Alice to secrecy.

His pain escalated because he knew Alice would never lie to him. "Do you think she went to Rapid City?"

She stared at him for a full minute. "I would not look for her in South Dakota. Perhaps Lindsey knows the truth."

Her Lakota soul had spoken to his, sending him a sign. He covered the distance between them and kissed her forehead before he set out to talk to his sister-in-law.

After being gone several hours on Saturday morning, Geena pulled up in front of her room at the Sleepy Time Motel in Laramie. It catered to families by providing rooms with a kitchenette and a crib, all the comforts of home for her and Lori.

She pulled the baby from the new car seat of her used Toyota and put her in the fold-up stroller she'd bought in Sundance with her own money. After grabbing the sack of ready-made formula from the front seat, she hurried inside the room to put Lori down for a nap with her bottle.

Geena had bought a newspaper and planned to look for live-in housekeeper jobs here. If there was no response in a few days, she'd head south to Fort Collins, Colorado. So far she'd found out nobody wanted a housekeeper with a baby.

Thanks to Alice, who'd driven her and Lori to the used-car dealership in Sundance on Wednesday, she'd been able to buy a second-hand car. She'd only brought their luggage and the carrycot with her. After thanking Alice profusely and waving her off, she was able to drive to the bank and withdraw some of her money. The rest she left in the account until she reached her final destination and had it transferred to a new bank.

Back at the ranch she'd left the keys on the dresser along with an envelope containing a letter to Colt and $7,000.00 in cash to repay him for everything. Alice had agreed to take over as temporary housekeeper until Colt found a new one. With that resolved, she'd set out to establish her new life with Lori away from the Floral Valley Ranch. Only distance and time would help heal the pain she'd been living through at the thought of never seeing Colt again.

While she scanned the want-ads, she heard a rap on the door. It was probably the maid bringing her some fresh towels. But when she opened it, she saw a tall man in a black cowboy hat who resembled Colt blocking the entrance. Yet he didn't look exactly like him because this man had a forbidding countenance and his eyes looked a furious black rather than a piercing hazel. His fists opened and closed at his sides.

"Colt—" Her hand went to her throat. She took a step back. "H-how did you find me?" Her voice faltered.

"Process of elimination," he bit out in a voice she wouldn't have recognized if she hadn't watched him say the words. "The man at the dealership in Sundance gave me a description of the car you bought and the license plate number. Lindsey told me you'd come to Laramie and were staying at a family-friendly motel. I figured as much, since you attended four years of college here. So I flew here and rented a car."

She shivered, because he would make a terrifying

adversary. "You shouldn't have come. I'm so sorry this has taken you away from the ranch unnecessarily. I told you everything in the letter and have tried to repay you in all the ways I could."

"You lied to me, Geena." His delivery was like a whiplash against her body. He hadn't heard anything she'd said.

"I've never lied to you—" she cried in defense. "I revere you too much to do that."

His mouth twisted cruelly. "What about my phone calls to you? 'Everything's fine,' you said. 'Don't worry about anything,' you insisted."

"But it was true!"

"No—" He almost spat the word. "You broke our contract. I trusted you. Now that trust is gone."

By now she was trembling, but she had to remain strong. "We agreed that my job was temporary while we determined if I was a good fit. But bringing Lori into your household changed the situation. You need a housekeeper, not a woman with a baby niece who requires extra attention and care. I became a burden, the last thing you asked for or deserved. Don't you understand how terrible I felt about doing that to you?"

His eyes narrowed to slits. "After assuring me on the phone that everything was fine, you left without saying one word to me," he accused her. "That's called a sin of omission. The worst kind." His voice grated with menace.

He wheeled around and headed for his rental car. She heard the tires squeal all the way out of the motel parking area.

She bit her teeth into the index finger of her hand.

Colt—what have I done?

This had to do with Cheryl, but she'd thought he and his ex-wife had come to an agreement before they'd divorced. He'd played it down when he'd told Geena about their problems and separation. But the white-faced rancher who'd just laid her out on the pavement had a lot more going on inside him than he'd allowed her to see until now.

Colt was in agony. Both Alice and Lindsey had seen that he'd been so affected by it, they'd told him the truth even though Geena had sworn them to secrecy. But she understood why because she was terrified by the change in him.

There was only one thing to do about it, and that was to go back and make him tell her exactly what was wrong.

To her relief, Lori had been a great little traveler on the way here. Geena had to hope her darling niece could handle the trip home. It would be a long drive. They probably wouldn't get to the ranch before late in the day, but it didn't matter. She needed to talk to Colt tonight!

Quick as she could, she packed them up and checked out at the motel office. Once on the road she headed north. Maybe Lori sensed something important was going on because she was an angel throughout the return trip. By the time they reached the ranch house, Geena was a complete wreck because she feared she wouldn't find Colt there. When she saw his truck, she practically passed out in relief.

But once she grabbed Lori and ran inside, he was nowhere to be found. The place was quiet as a tomb. She hurried back to her car with Lori and drove to Travis's house. He answered her knock and looked shocked to see her standing there with Lori in her arms.

"I thought you were in Laramie."

Lindsey joined him, equally surprised to find her at their door. "Geena?"

"I came home to talk to Colt, but he's not in the house. Do you know where he is?"

Travis eyed her speculatively. "I do, but—"

"I have to find him—" she broke in, cutting him off. One brow lifted. "How badly?"

They weren't brothers for nothing. He knew his big brother was hurting. Right then her love for Travis grew in leaps. "It's a matter of life and death to me."

He stared at her. "Life and death, huh?"

"Yes. We've had a terrible misunderstanding. I—I'm in love with him."

His eyes flickered. "If you'd said anything else…" He gave her a hug. "After he flew back from Laramie, I heard him tell Hank he was headed for the sheepherder's shelter in the high meadow and he didn't care what in the devil happened while he was away. No one was to know where he'd gone or when he'd be back. You'll have to get there on horseback."

"I know. When we went riding, he pointed it out to me. Do you think if I called Alice, she'd tend Lori for me tonight?"

"Why do that when you've got me?" Lindsey questioned. Geena could hardly believe what she'd just heard. "I can take care of her tonight. Abby often sleeps in her carrycot. We'll put Lori in the crib."

"You'd do that for me?"

"After the way you've been waiting on me, it's my chance to pay you back." She reached for Lori. "We'll take good care of her till you get back."

"You're terrific." She hugged Lindsey and gave the

baby a kiss. "I've got plenty of ready-made formula and diapers in the car."

"I'll get everything. Travis, honey? Will you saddle Carrot Top for her? There's enough daylight left for her to make it without problem."

"Sure I will. Come on. Let's get you on your way. I've only seen Colt bad one other time, but it was nothing compared to today. I hardly recognized him as my own flesh and blood."

Geena could top that. She didn't know the fierce stranger who'd left the motel in such turmoil.

"Thank you both for this."

Lindsey put an arm around her. In a whisper she said, "Colt can be scary when he's upset, but since you survived prison, I'm backing you."

Geena hugged her hard before hurrying after Travis.

"What in the hell are you making all that racket for, Titus? You've sniffed mountain lions and coyotes before."

Colt was trying to get the lantern to work. If it was broken, then he'd have no light until morning, but it didn't matter. The shelter was nothing more than a lean-to for when a hand got stranded in a blizzard. You could barely turn around in it.

He couldn't remember the last time the furnishings had been replaced, but that didn't matter either. Colt liked it this way. The tiny camp stove still worked and there was a pan to fry fish. What more could a man want with a mountain stream full of trout at his door?

All he required at the moment was the cot. One of these days it was going to collapse, but he'd worry about that when it happened.

By now Titus was at the door, yelping and scratching his paws against the wood in desperation. Colt knew he didn't need to go out any more tonight. "What in blazes has gotten into you?" He put the lantern on the floor and walked over to him. That's when he heard the neigh from more than one horse.

Anger consumed him that someone had ridden all the way up here. Unless an emergency had happened to his mother, he'd warned Travis to keep everyone away! Without taking care, he flung the door open. In the process the top hinge gave way so the door hung on a slant, but by now he was distracted because he'd seen someone dismounting the other horse.

Carrot Top?

Titus took off. Colt let him go because all of a sudden Geena came striding toward him, sending every thought flying. She was dressed in her designer jeans and cowboy boots. Outlining her beautiful body was the white Western shirt she'd bought in Sundance. The night breeze fluttered the ends of her hair and carried her fragrance. It almost knocked him over with recent memories of holding her in his arms while he buried his face in her dark brown mane.

He swallowed hard, thinking this might be a hallucination. "What are you doing here?"

"What do you think?"

This was the same female who'd faced him in the kitchen on that first night, but there were differences. This woman was the finished version. Complete. Full of confidence.

"How did you get here so fast?"

"I drove over the speed limit, just like you do."

Colt couldn't fathom it. "But that means you and Lori would've had to leave Laramie right after I did—"

"Yup. My niece is a fantastic traveler."

"Where is she?"

"Lindsey's tending her overnight."

His heart raced. He was too astounded to see Geena standing in front of him to question anything else. She'd come all the way on horseback and now darkness was falling over the mountainside. "You shouldn't have made the trip."

She put her hands on womanly hips, defeating him with her feminine charm. "Then I've come in vain?"

"I didn't say that."

"You called me a liar. I was called that once before and spent thirteen months confined before the truth was uncovered. I'm not about to spend one more night in pain for something I didn't do. Not when I've been accused by a man I admire more than any man in existence. So explain to me what you meant."

Colt couldn't take much more of this. "Let's just say you're not the person I thought you were."

"That's interesting. What kind of a person am I? I tried to do my best as your housekeeper. When I got the money the state gave me, I was able to pay you back. Of course there's no way to recompense you for your kindness, but I returned everything I could. As I told you in the letter, Alice only agreed to pinch hit. I hoped you wouldn't disapprove and thought she was a good choice for a replacem—"

"Why did you leave without discussing it with me first?" he broke in without apology.

Geena took a step closer to him. "Because I was

afraid that generous streak in your nature would prompt you to ask me to stay on longer."

"Would that be such a terrible penance?"

"Yes."

He bit down so hard he came close to slicing his tongue off. "I should have realized that after prison, the isolation of the ranch would be too much for you, too."

"You mean like it was for Cheryl? Come on, Colt. You don't really put me in the same category with her. What else did she do to you I don't know about? It's truth time."

"She lied from the moment we met."

"How?"

"By telling me she wanted to be a rancher's wife. I bought it and ended up paying for it."

"She didn't lie, Colt. She loved you and wanted you. I have no doubt she intended to be the wife of your dreams, but she found out it was a lifestyle she couldn't handle. She was a city girl, and deep down you knew it!"

He couldn't fight her logic.

"I, on the other hand, can't get enough of the ranch or the owner. Didn't you listen to a word I said the other night? I told you I thought the Sundance Kid was a fool not to have settled down right here."

Colt shook his head, afraid to believe her. "I never asked you to leave, Geena. I didn't want that damned contract in the first place."

Her breath was coming faster. He could hear it. "So what are you saying? That you want me to stay on as your permanent housekeeper and keep Lori with me until I've died of old age? That's what you told the sister at the convent."

"I said that so she wouldn't give you any grief about taking Lori home with us that day."

"Even though your ploy worked, you didn't mean any of it, did you?"

"You know damn well I did."

"You swear too much, do you know that?"

"Geena—"

"Well, as grateful as I am to you for everything, I'm sorry, because the answer is still no."

"That's what I thought. So why in the hell did you come back?"

"You really don't get it, do you?" she said in an emotional voice.

"Get what?" He'd had as much as he could take.

"Ooh— Sometimes you build those walls so high around you, nobody can climb over them. I'll say this once.

"I love everything and everyone on the Floral Valley Ranch. Everyone! Did you hear that? I mean *you*, Colt Brannigan. I'm madly, desperately in love with you! Don't you see that being your housekeeper would only be half a loaf? I want the whole thing with a wedding ring, nights under the stars like this, babies, grandchildren.

"You'll probably think I'm crazy, but from the moment I saw your ad in the paper, it seemed to have special meaning for me. But I'm afraid your heart died with Cheryl. If you think I'm going to stay around here for any other reason, then you don't know me at all. If I did that, then my heart would die, too, so I'm not going to let that happen.

"I want love in my life. I found out in prison that I need it. If it can't be you, then I have to believe there's someone else out there for me and Lori. I refuse to let my heart turn into a dried-up prune like yours."

Before he could think, she turned and dashed toward her horse, but Colt was faster and caught her in his arms before she could put her foot in the stirrup. "Feel *this*." He grasped her hand and pressed it against his heart. "Now tell me it's dried up."

"Colt—"

"I've been in love with you from the beginning, Geena. You know I have."

"I wanted to believe it."

"Then believe this." He molded her to his body and kissed that mouth he craved. "For weeks I've wanted to tell you, but I thought I'd give you more time to adapt to the ranch so you'd never want to leave."

"I always dreamed of living on a ranch. I'm a South Dakota girl. Don't you know it almost killed me to leave you?" she admitted, finding every part of his face and throat to devour. They clung with a ferocity that told him this time was forever for both of them.

"I want you for my wife. The family—everyone— adores you. I should have asked you to marry me when we brought Lori home. I've wasted too much time. I want us both to adopt her so we can be her legal parents. I'm crazy about her, too." He kissed her long and thoroughly. "Forgive me for today."

"If you'll forgive me for leaving without telling you. I never meant to hurt you, Colt. You're my very life. I poured out my heart to you in that letter."

"I know. I felt it and was humbled by the words. Marry me soon, Geena. We don't have time to waste."

She flashed him a seducing half smile. "I agree. Let's go somewhere private and discuss it."

"I'd invite you in, but this lean-to is ready to cave at any second. While you ride on Digger with me, we'll discuss wedding plans until we reach the house. But after we arrive, there'll be no more talk. I love you, Geena. When I got home and found you gone...well, you don't want to know what it did to me."

"Oh darling—don't ever stop loving me," she begged. "No quarter asked, remember?"

"None given, my love. That's a promise."

EPILOGUE

"AND so, by the power vested in me, I now pronounce you man and wife. What God has joined together, let no man put asunder."

In the next breath Colt kissed Geena with such hunger, she was blushing by the time she heard the pastor clear his throat.

"Darling—"

"I heard him," Colt murmured against her lips, "but I have the right to kiss my new wife for as long as I want in my own house. I swear I'll love you forever, Geena."

"You think I don't love you the same way?" she cried softly, out of breath.

His brothers surrounded them. "Time to break this up, bro, so we can kiss the bride." There was laughter from the guests as Hank and Travis welcomed her into the family. Pretty soon everyone gathered round and Geena had never been so happy in her life. Pictures were taken.

The ranch house, decorated with fall flowers for the three o'clock ceremony, was filled with at least a hundred friends that included the ranch hands, staff and relatives. Everyone milled around eating the delicious food, laughing and talking.

Geena had invited Kellie, who'd struck up a conversation with Mandy over in the corner. Colt's mother sat near the fireplace with Ina. She looked stunning in an off-white lace suit Geena had picked out for her. Geena wore a white chiffon-and-lace dress that fell to the knee.

Lindsey wore a soft blue suit and took over tending Lori in the stroller while her baby was upstairs in bed asleep. Their two little girls would grow up together. Nothing could have thrilled Geena more. The fact that Hank had invited Mandy to the ceremony gave Geena hope there might be another wedding one day soon.

Lieutenant Crowther was the last to come up and congratulate Geena. His eyes looked suspiciously bright. "This is the kind of ending you wish for every person who's ever been wrongfully accused."

Tears trickled from Geena's eyes as she kissed his cheek. "If there's ever anything I can do for you, you know where to find me."

"I'll remember that."

"We both mean it," Colt said in an emotional voice, shaking the detective's hand. "Because of you, we've found our happiness."

After he left, Colt grasped Geena's shoulders. "The car is packed. Let's go while Lori is being distracted. If she sees us leave, she'll have a meltdown."

"You're right."

Without anyone being prepared for it, Colt edged Geena toward the hallway. At the last second, Geena tossed her bouquet to a surprised Mandy before they slipped out the front door and hurried to the car Laura Brannigan had driven before she became ill.

Colt started the engine and they took off down the drive. He reached for Geena's hand and squeezed it all the way to the highway. "Only a few more miles until we're alone."

"You're driving over the speed limit, darling."

His eyes blazed with love for her. "Henpecking me already?"

"Yes. I want us to live for a long time."

"I want that, too, since I'm planning on us having another baby by next year. Let's hope our beach honeymoon is productive."

Geena blushed while her heart leaped. "Boy or girl?"

"It doesn't matter. Lori Lou has made me hungry for more."

"She's crazy about you, Colt."

"The feeling's mutual. I was praying she was your niece."

"Why?"

"Besides making you happy, I knew it would alter your plans for the future. That was good, because I intended your future to be with me. I could see you and me together as husband and wife, with more family to come besides Lori. For the first time since I can remember, my life feels complete. That's your doing, darling."

To her surprise, he pulled to the side of the road and drew her into his arms. They kissed long and hard.

When he finally relinquished her lips, she said, "You know the old saying that when God closes a door, he always opens a window? That year in prison was my window because it led me to you. Those thirteen months weren't a waste. They taught me that every moment of life is precious. You're precious to me, Colt."

He crushed her to him. "Welcome to the Floral Valley Ranch and my heart, Mrs. Brannigan."

* * * * *

COMING NEXT MONTH from Harlequin® Romance

#4327 NANNY FOR THE MILLIONAIRE'S TWINS
First Time Dads!
Susan Meier
Chance Montgomery lays the past to rest with the help of his adorable twin babies and their beautiful nanny, Tory.

#4328 SLOW DANCE WITH THE SHERIFF
The Larkville Legacy
Nikki Logan
Ex-ballerina Ellie leaves Manhattan behind to look for answers in sleepy Larkville, but instead finds dreamy county sheriff, Jed Jackson....

#4329 THE NAVY SEAL'S BRIDE
Heroes Come Home
Soraya Lane
Navy SEAL Tom is struggling with civilian life. Can beautiful teacher Caitlin crack the walls around this soldier's battle-worn heart?

#4330 ALWAYS THE BEST MAN
Fiona Harper
Before their best friends' wedding is over, will Ice-cool Damien realize he's the best man for bubbly bridesmaid Zoe?

#4331 HOW THE PLAYBOY GOT SERIOUS
The McKenna Brothers
Shirley Jump
Playboy Riley discovers that it will take more than his blue eyes and easy smile to impress feisty waitress Stace....

#4332 NEW YORK'S FINEST REBEL
Trish Wylie
Sparks fly when fashionista Jo realizes her sworn enemy—the infuriatingly attractive cop, Daniel Brannigan—has moved in next door!

You can find more information on upcoming Harlequin® titles, free excerpts and more at www.Harlequin.com.

HRCNM0712

REQUEST YOUR FREE BOOKS!
2 FREE NOVELS PLUS 2 FREE GIFTS!

Harlequin
Romance

From the Heart, For the Heart

Discover an enchanting duet filled with glitz,
glamour and passionate love from

Melanie Milburne

The twin sisters **everyone's** *talking about!*

Separated by secrets…

Having grown up in different families, Gisele and Sienna live lives
that are worlds apart. Then a very public revelation
propels them into the world's eye….

Drawn together by scandal!

Now the sisters have found each other—but are they at risk of losing
their hearts to the two men who are determined to peel back
the layers of their glittering facades?

Find out in

DESERVING OF HIS DIAMONDS?
Available July 24

ENEMIES AT THE ALTAR
Available August 21

USA TODAY *bestselling author Lynne Graham brings you a brand-new story of passion and drama.*

THE SECRETS SHE CARRIED

"DON'T play games with me," she urged, breathing in deeply and slowly, nostrils flaring in dismay at the familiar spicy scent of his designer aftershave.

The smell of him, so achingly familiar, unleashed a tide of memories. But Cristo had not made a commitment to her, had not done anything to make her feel secure and had never once mentioned love or the future. At the end of the day, in spite of all her precautions, he had still walked away untouched while she had been crushed in the process.

The knowledge that she had meant so little to him that he had ditched her to marry another woman still burned like acid inside her.

"Maybe I'm hoping you'll finally come clean," Cristo murmured levelly.

Erin turned her head, smooth brow indented with a frown as she struggled to recall the conversation and get back into it again. "Come clean about what?"

Cristo pulled off the road into a layby before he responded. "I found out what you were up to while you were working for me at the Mobila spa."

Erin twisted her entire body around to look at him, crystalline eyes flaring bright, her rising tension etched in the taut set of her heart-shaped face. "What do you mean… what I was up to?"

Cristo looked at her levelly, ebony dark eyes cool and opaque as frosted glass. "You were stealing from me."

"I am not a thief," Erin repeated doggedly, although an alarm bell had gone off in her head the instant he mentioned the theft and sale of products from the store.

"I have the proof," Cristo retorted crisply. "You can't talk or charm your way out of this, Erin—"

"I'm not interested in charming you. I'm not the same woman I was when we were together," Erin countered curtly, for what he had done to her had toughened her. There was nothing like surviving an unhappy love affair to build self-knowledge and character, she reckoned painfully. He had broken her heart, taught her how fragile she was, left her bitter and humiliated. But she had had to pick herself up again fast once she'd discovered that she was pregnant.

Cristo is going to make Erin pay back what he believes she stole—in whatever way he demands.... But little does he know that Erin's about to drop two very important bombshells!

Pick up a copy of THE SECRETS SHE CARRIED by Lynne Graham, available August 2012 from Harlequin Presents®.

Harlequin® Super Romance®

Enjoy a month of compelling, emotional stories, including a poignant new tale of love lost and found from

Sarah Mayberry

When Angela Bartlett loses her best friend to a rare heart condition, it seems only natural that she step in and help widower and friend Michael Young. The last thing she expects is to find herself falling for him....

Within Reach

Available August 7!

Find more great stories this month from
Harlequin® Superromance® at

www.Harlequin.com

HSRSM71795

Harlequin®

ROMANTIC
SUSPENSE

CINDY DEES

takes you on a wild journey to find the truth
in her new miniseries

Code X

Aiden McKay is more than just an ordinary man. As part of
an elite secret organization, Aiden was genetically enhanced
to increase his lung capacity and spend extended time under
water. He is a committed soldier, focused and dedicated
to his job. But when Aiden saves impulsive free spirit
Sunny Jordan from drowning she promptly overturns his
entire orderly, solitary world.

As the danger creeps closer, Adien soon realizes Sunny is the
target…but can he save her in time?

Breathless Encounter

Find out this August!

Look out for a reader-favorite bonus story included in each
Harlequin Romantic Suspense book this August!

www.Harlequin.com

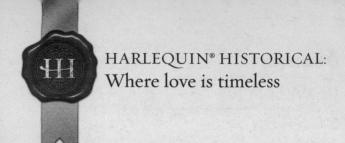

HARLEQUIN® HISTORICAL:
Where love is timeless

Fan-favorite author

JILLIAN HART

brings you a timeless tale of faith and love in

Montana Bride

Willa Conner learned a long time ago that love is a fairy tale. She's been left widowed, pregnant and penniless, and her last hope is the stranger who answers her ad for a husband.

Austin Dermot, a hardworking Montana blacksmith, doesn't know what to expect from a mail-order bride. It certainly isn't the brave, beautiful, but scarred young woman who cautiously steps off the train....

Trust won't come easily for Willa—it's hard for her to believe she's worthy of true love. But she doesn't need to worry about that, because this is just a marriage of convenience...isn't it?

Can two strangers be a match made in the West?

Find out this August!